Mystic Warrior

A Novel Beyond Time and Space

Edwin Harkness Spina

ISBN: 0-9745871-0-9

LCCN 2003113245

Publishing Consultant: Sylvia Hemmerly
Interior Design and Typesetting: Publishing Professionals, Port Richey, FL
Cover Design: Mythic Design Studio, Glover, VT

Printed in Canada

The paper used in this publication meets the minimum requirements of the American National Standard for Information Sciences—Permanence of Paper for Printed Library Materials, ANSI Z39.48-1984.

Acknowledgements

First, I would like to thank my Mom, who is always there for me. During a particularly bad stretch—when I was flat broke, without a car, being evicted from my apartment, my company going out of business, and my girlfriend breaking up with me—I called my Mom to tell her I was moving in with her. She didn't ask any questions, other than "What time will you be arriving?" I wrote the majority of *Mystic Warrior* during the time period I lived with her.

Next, I would like to thank my editor, Willy Mathes, who helped bring this story to life, Jamon Walker, who designed the cover, and my consultant, Sylvia Hemmerly, who introduced me to both of these professionals and who provided much expert guidance.

Also, I would like to thank my friends and colleagues who read various drafts of this work and provided critical feedback. They are (in alphabetical order): Cherokee Paul McDonald, Curtis Lake, Dara Dubinet, Darnella Cordier, Doug McCraw, Ellen Randolph, Fonda Byrns, Joan Roth, Joanne Kilmartin, Ray Casper, Rick McBride, and Tommy Rosa.

A special warm thank you to the many others who offered me support and advice. To name each of you would be a book in itself.

Edwin Harkness Spina

The thing that has been is that which shall be; and that which has been done is that which shall be done; and there is nothing new under the sun. Whosoever speaks and says, Look, this is new, should know that it already has been in the ages which were before us.

—Ecclesiastes 1:9-10

Prologue

△ △ △

We are not human beings having a spiritual experience,
we are spiritual beings having a human experience.
—Pierre Teilhard de Chardin

Summer 1976

EIGHT-YEAR OLD Alec Thorn paused to catch his breath as he neared the top of Waimoku Falls on East Maui. He sat down on a well-worn rock and took a sip from the water bottle that he carried on his belt. Though the sun had not yet risen, he could make out the shapes of the hala trees, with their long, spiny leaves and aerial roots, in the predawn light.

Alec inhaled deeply. The rich smells of the hala fruit and the sweet scent of the golden and pink plumeria flowers filled his nostrils. The sound of the water cascading down Mount Haleakala soothed him. It was the last day of his family's trip and he yearned to experience the beauty of this place one more time, alone, without distraction.

Alec closed his eyes to feel the energy, sensing its intensity. He couldn't tell: was it inside him or outside? At that moment, it was both; everything was connected and he was part of it. A sense of wonder overtook Alec. *Why am I me? Why not a water bottle?* Instantly, he was no longer in his body, but watching a skinny, young boy with brown hair sitting on a rock. The boy wore a striped knit shirt, baggy shorts and white Converse All-Star basketball sneakers that were covered with mud.

Hovering overhead, silently observing the youth, Alec's mind was at peace before terror overtook him. *He was the boy.* He immediately popped back into his body.

1

Inside his head, Alec heard a gentle, comforting voice, *"Don't be afraid. You know how to do this."*

Though eager to try it again, fear still paralyzed him. The reassuring voice returned, *"This is how you travel to distant worlds."*

Alec listened to the voice and allowed himself to relax. He let go of his fear and was free again. Floating above the greenery, he could see the sun emerging from the ocean to the east.

"Alec!" shouted his father. "Where are you?"

He was jerked suddenly back into his body. "Over here."

He watched his father appear from behind a clump of bamboo that obscured the hiking trail. "What're you doing? You've got your mother all worried. You can't take off without asking."

"Dad, I was flying," replied Alec.

His father looked at him blankly and said, "Let's go."

"Really, Dad." The boy looked up at his father with utter sincerity, but could tell by the look on his face that he was not listening.

"Hurry up or we'll be late."

Alec picked up his water bottle and followed his father down the mountain, knowing it would be a long time before he would get to go back.

1

△ △ △

Summer 2001

JIM KRAMER WAS pulling his white Buick Century out of the FCC parking garage on 12th Street SW at 7:15 PM, when his cell phone rang. "Hello."

"Jim, it's Alec Thorn. "I'm not interrupting anything, am I?"

"Not at all. I just left the office."

"Is our approval still scheduled for tomorrow?" Alec asked, barely able to disguise his anxiety.

"Ye-e-s," replied Jim, in a drawn-out, teasing tone he hoped would inspire some confidence in this cautious, yet bright, young entrepreneur.

"You're sure? No other hoops to jump through?" asked Alec, always leery of bureaucracy.

"Relax, Alec. Your wireless application will be officially licensed by noon tomorrow." He laughed and added, "If I have to, I'll *personally* type up the certificate."

"Thanks. I don't mean to pester you, but there's a lot riding on this," Alec said, his tone a mixture of both gratitude and nervousness.

"I know. It's nice to see a small company get a break for a change. That's why I pushed so hard." Indeed, though he wasn't obliged to, Jim had logged dozens of hours of overtime over the previous three weeks to help ensure Alec's license approval path was made as smooth as possible.

"Thanks, again. I really appreciate your help, Jim," he replied, beginning to breathe somewhat easier.

"You're welcome. Look, enjoy your evening. I'll call you to-morrow." He punched the end button on his cell phone, feeling a sense of satisfaction at having helped Alec navigate his way through the FCC's daunting application process.

Now several blocks from his downtown Washington, D.C. office, Jim Kramer headed out of the city in light traffic. Smoothly he accelerated along Independence Avenue towards the Lincoln Memorial.

Feeling sleepy, he switched on his car radio and then checked his watch. It was only 7:30 PM. *Damn, I shouldn't be tired at* **this** *hour*. He turned his eyes back to the road, but soon his eyelids closed. Seconds passed. Abruptly, he forced them open, as he steered his way around the cloverleaf onto the Memorial Bridge.

Again, his eyes closed and the sound of the radio faded. His left hand slipped from the steering wheel and the car veered head-long into the pedestrian walkway. Kramer awoke just as it crashed through the railing of the bridge.

Flying through the cool night air, the car momentarily resem-bled a silent, oversized metal toy being tossed from a bridge, before plummeting 30 feet towards the Potomac. Kramer's head slammed into the windshield as his Buick struck the water.

2

△ △ △

ALEC THORN BOLTED upright, his thin, wiry body flush with perspiration, his hazel eyes peering into the darkness as he fought to get his bearings. The sound of his girlfriend's exasperated sigh helped him regain his focus. He was still in bed.

"*Another* dream?" Reggie asked, her tone laden with dismay. "The same one?"

He nodded, a dazed look evident atop the bags under his eyes. She shook her head in frustration and coldly turned away from him. It was the third time in a week Alec had woken her up with his nightmare, and both her body language and tone of voice told him she was more than tired of it.

He remained sitting up, but closed his eyes again, trying to make sense of his dream, not wanting to be interrupted. *Was I responsible?* This time, Alec could picture Jim Kramer in his car, hanging up after speaking with him. *The approval was as good as signed, he'd said—he had actually joked about it! There was no way Kramer could have fallen asleep at the wheel only minutes after I was talking with him!*

Reggie interrupted his thoughts by getting up out of bed in a huff. "I'm leaving!"

Alec turned to look at her, as she began to get dressed and despite her obvious resentment toward him she looked attractive. Her shoulder length, light brown hair cascaded sensually over her shoulders, starkly contrasting alluringly with her starched white shirt and medium gray suit. He weighed saying some comforting words against continuing with his dream-reflections, but she started out of the bedroom without another word. He hesitated. In

5

his dream, he'd nearly reached the point where Kramer had crashed, feeling somehow that he himself was responsible for this key player's mysterious death. He *had* to know what happened, what or who caused this; but, for the moment, Reggie was angry —more than usual. Alec threw off the bed covers and started to move toward the bedroom door.

"Don't bother to get up!" she yelled from the kitchen. He caught up with her, but she ignored him as she poured a glass of orange juice. After a few moments, Reggie faced him and blurted out, "You need to work this out yourself. You're obsessed with it! The police said his death was an *accident*! Can't you let it *go*?" Her glare and tone of voice stripped any vestiges of sleepiness from him. "You work eighty hours a week on your new company. We *never* go out and even when we sleep together, you wake me up with your goddamn nightmare! You don't need a girlfriend; you need a shrink!"

Wisely, he kept quiet. *She's a Yale graduate—she could be right.*

"Listen, Alec," Reggie said, pointing her finger in his face, "I'm going to visit my parents this weekend." Her reddened face screamed at him just how agitated she was. "Unless you get yourself straightened out, don't ever bother calling me again!"

A huge lump formed in his throat. He had only dated Reggie for three months; what he needed now were friends and support. Still, he knew it wasn't fair to expect her to deal with *both* the financial roller coaster he was on *and* this series of hellish nightmares.

The door slammed shut behind her. Alec Thorn closed his eyes, took a deep breath and exhaled slowly. He turned towards the clock that read 7:01 AM. He was late for work.

3

△ △ △

Erica Buenavista sat at Mezzaluna's outdoor cafe watching the crowd. It was almost noon and the beautiful people were waking up and filing in for brunch.

Taking out her compact, she inspected her appearance, admiring the blonde Teutonic features she had inherited from her mother. Seated outdoors looking onto Ocean Boulevard, Erica looked stylish wearing a red silk blouse, a beige skirt that fell just above her knee and expensive flats from Italy. Her sunlit golden hair fell gracefully over her shoulders. She prided herself on her superb fashion sense and enjoyed her visits to South Beach, where she could keep her finger on the pulse of new fashion trends.

Within minutes, she attracted the attention of two gentlemen wearing lightweight European suits. They casually approached her table and stood side-by-side, openly admiring her.

"Are you alone?" asked the tall one, with a slight accent. "Please join us for lunch."

Smiling demurely, she identified his accent as German. Dressed too well to be tourists and overly confident, they were more likely to be real estate investors. "Thank you, but I'm waiting for someone." She turned away to dismiss them. The men retreated.

Erica had chosen her outfit to exude an image of wealth and nobility and was pleased that it was working. The right clothing, she knew, could be a useful tool to manipulate people.

Glancing at her Cartier Tank watch, she suspected that Hawke was late. Such insubordination would have infuriated her, but checking the time more carefully, she realized he was not due for another 15 minutes.

After taking a sip from her glass of Santa Margherita Pinot Grigio, Erica spotted Hawke, a block away, walking toward her, striding casually along in his trademark self-assured manner. Dressed appropriately for Miami in a beige short sleeve dress shirt and matching linen slacks, he blended in with the crowd. In her mind, Hawke was the classic American cowboy—no different from the *gauchos* of her native Argentina. His manner was crude by her standards, but she admired his rugged good looks. Though their business often dictated that they not attract attention, today was an exception. Hawke's tone of voice on the phone indicated he had succeeded; this was a moment to celebrate.

He approached her table and sat down. "I ran into a few problems, but everything is fixed and we're back on schedule." He smiled as he looked around, checking to see they weren't in ear-shot of anyone. "The device is in a safe place."

"What about the scientist, Federov?" Erica asked.

"He's in a safe place, too."

"Alive?"

"We didn't need him anymore," he said dryly.

"Any other problems?" Her eyes rose slightly, as she wondered what other information he might be withholding.

"It cost more money than we budgeted," he said matter-of-factly, watching for her reaction.

"How much more?" she asked, annoyed that her plans had not gone smoothly.

"A hundred-fifty grand," he answered.

"What happened?" Her question carried a slightly accusing tone.

"There are criminals all *over* the place," he shot back defensively. "Some of them thought we were moving in on their smuggling operations."

"Where were the ex-KGB guys we paid for protection?" she asked, not hiding her exasperation.

"Those chicken shits wouldn't go past the Kazakhstan border."

Erica tensed. The object, she'd explained clearly to him, was to get the device out of the country *without* attracting attention. Hawke's heavy-handedness could have ruined everything, but that was his nature. In times of trouble, he went back to what he did best—shoot first and ask questions later.

"So, I wonder what you decided to do?" she pondered aloud.

"I remembered what you said about not looking for trouble," Hawke replied. "But they were welshing on the deal. I told them that they would get paid when everything was out of the country, including me. They wanted more money."

"And . . .?"

"I got them to throw in six stinger missiles for another hundred-fifty grand." He smiled, proud of his negotiating skills.

"You weren't supposed to be shopping for more weapons," Erica chided, not impressed with his business judgment. She paused for a moment to consider the irony of ex-KGB agents selling American-made weapons, a common practice in an industry that knew no borders. She took a breath and let it out slowly. "You could have jeopardized everything."

Hawke waited for her anger to pass. "It was a good deal and it got them off my back."

"Where are the stingers?" she asked, still angry.

"That's where the problem came up. Less than 100 klicks down the road, I had to deal with the criminals again."

"Go on," she said.

"Well," he began, "they blockaded the road and wouldn't let me pass. I think they assumed I had drugs or weapons in the truck and they wanted to search it—"

"Which is why you weren't supposed to be shopping for other weapons," she railed. "What happened next?" Her ire was on full display for Hawke, but he ignored it and continued with his story.

"I told them they couldn't search the truck. They insisted. I got pissed."

Erica took a deep breath. "And then?"

"I shot one bastard right between the eyes and then pointed my gun at the guy giving the orders. In about two seconds, six guys with AK-47s showed up. It was a standoff."

Hawke smiled, quite pleased with himself. "I made him an offer. If he would quit screwing around with me, I would let him have the stingers. If he didn't—well, I wasn't sure who would win the battle, but I guaranteed him that he was personally going to lose."

Hawke paused to relish his story. "They took the stingers, but let me through."

Though such close calls often made dealing with Hawke challenging, Erica was relieved that he accomplished the task, however crudely. "Everything is set then?"

"Yeah. It's hidden underground. I can give directions to our buyer once we're paid. Until then no one could possibly find it."

"You're sure?"

Hawke leaned back and folded his arms in a stance of self-assuredness. "Not a chance," he bragged. "The cave entrance is camouflaged by the holographic projection. All anyone would see if they happened to pass by is solid rock. Even the high-resolution satellites couldn't find it, no matter what frequency they use to probe the area."

She let Hawke's words sink in. Taking a last sip of wine, a hint of a smile formed on her lips as she stood up. "Let's go. We have work to do."

4

When the student is ready, the teacher will appear.
—Zen Proverb

THAT EVENING WHILE driving home, Alec Thorn's thoughts returned to his early morning argument with Reggie. He was glad that he'd been so busy at the office that he didn't have time to brood about it. *What does she want from me? She knows I have a business to run,* he reflected, as he pulled into the shopping center on North Federal Highway to pick up his shirts at the dry cleaners. *Doesn't she realize we'll be able to travel to Paris and all the other places she dreams about as soon as I get my company going? Maybe she'd be better off with some doctor or lawyer!* He paid for his shirts and left the cleaners. Still feeling at a loss to understand Reggie, Thorn noticed a florist shop only two stores down. It was not well marked, but he was surprised that he'd never noticed it before. *Flowers might help lessen Reggie's anger at me,* he thought, still perplexed as to how to deal with his apparently unappreciated girlfriend.

Thorn entered the shop and was amazed at the variety of flowers and plants inside. Many of them he had never seen before. It seemed odd that after countless visits to the same shopping center, such a shop should be hidden in plain sight.

A petite brunette in her mid-thirties, wearing a full-length flower print silk dress, emerged from the back to welcome him. She smiled and greeted him with a pleasant European accent. "Hello. Please feel free to look around. I can answer any questions you might have."

Though Thorn felt a sense of familiarity, he didn't recognize the woman. Her green eyes were unusual—they seemed to change color as he watched, but even that wasn't it. *Something else,* he thought. *Perhaps I've seen her walking around the shopping center before.* He let it go and stared at the magnificent array of color surrounding him. "I've never seen so many exotic flowers. Your shop is beautiful!"

"Thank you. I try to keep a good variety. My clients often have need of something unusual."

"I'm sorry I never came in before. Don't mind my saying so, but your shop is not well marked. With a little promotion, this place would be packed with customers."

"Those that need to, find their way here," she casually replied. "Like you."

"Like me? Is it that obvious I need help?" he asked, trying to hide his sadness.

"Yes." She paused, staring at him for an unusually long few moments, before continuing. "You have big problems, which is why you came."

Thorn smiled. "You're right—girlfriend problems."

She grinned while shaking her head. "That's the *least* of your worries."

A puzzled look replaced Thorn's smile. It was not his practice to share his problems with every florist he met and he decided not to start with her, no matter how perceptive she seemed.

"Don't worry. I have just the thing for you," she interjected. "Wait here while I get it ready." She turned away from him and disappeared into the back.

Thorn was too confused to stop her. He decided to wait. A few minutes later, she returned with a small perfume bottle. "Smell this," she said, holding it out toward him.

Thorn bent over to sniff the faint floral aroma that had subtle traces of herbs and spices. "What is it?"

"Never mind," she replied, ignoring his question. "Starting tonight, I want you to put a drop of this oil behind each of your ears before you go to bed for the next three nights. Also, I want you to fill a vase with water and leave it on your night table. Come back and see me in three days and bring the oil and the water."

"This is going to help me?" asked Thorn.

"Just do it." Though her tone was not demanding, it was obvious she had no desire to entertain or discuss it with him.

She handed the bottle to Thorn, but rather than release it, she clasped the bottle and his hand between her two hands and held them tightly. Her eyes lost their focus, as she gazed off into the distance. As quickly as she started, she stopped and refocused her eyes on Thorn.

"A man with a hat is going to offer you a deal. Don't take it." She looked at him plainly, quite matter-of-factly, as though she'd just told him that since it was raining outside, he should take an umbrella with him.

"Who? What deal? What are you talking about?!" Standing in front of her dumbfounded, he couldn't tell whether she was actually tuning in to something real or just pulling his leg.

"That's all I got," she calmly replied. "Don't worry—you'll know what to do."

Thorn surveyed her for a few moments, intrigued by the sureness of her words and actions. *No harm in trying,* he mused to himself. "All right, then. What do I owe you?"

"Pay me after you see the results."

The savvy businessman in Thorn emerged. "How can you stay in business if you don't charge anything for your merchandise?"

"Don't worry about me, right now. A lot of people are very envious of you. You've got to protect yourself until you understand what you're dealing with."

Could she be right? And if she were, how could she know anything about me? He stared blankly at her, unsure of what to make of her.

"Also, stop and get some vitamins. You're not eating right and you need them to help your body deal with the stress. Your thyroid is out of balance."

"How do you know I need vitamins? Are you a nutritionist?"

"From the colors in your aura."

"My what?"

"Enough already." Her face tightened slightly, before it relaxed into a broad, gentle smile. "Look, I have to close up and go home. I'll see you in three days."

Thorn left, mystified, amazed and without the flowers that he had originally come in for.

5

△ △ △

THE NEXT MORNING, Thorn arrived at his office just past 8 AM. After stopping at his desk to check his email, he went down to the kitchen for a cup of tea. From there he could see Carol Jordan, his vice president, on the phone.

The sight of Carol always helped to cheer Thorn up. As usual, the five foot four inch, wavy-haired brunette was dressed impeccably in a beige skirt, white blouse and navy blazer. Thorn had once thought to tell her to loosen up, but it struck him as a perverse form of reverse discrimination. With no dress code, the programmers typically wore knit shirts and jeans. To tell her that she was dressed too tastefully would be absurd.

Thorn saw Carol dressed less conservatively only once. He ran into her and her abusive husband at a nightclub before her divorce. In an alluring, tight, stretchy black dress, she was stunning. He often felt the sexual tension between them and sensed that the feelings might be mutual. In the back of his mind, though, he knew he should never abuse his position as her boss. Besides, it was much harder to find a qualified VP than a girlfriend. She remained a trusted confidante, despite the temptation he occasionally felt.

"Sleep late?" she asked after she'd hung up the phone and walked into the office kitchen.

Thorn forced himself to smile and nod. Normally he would have responded with a wisecrack, but he wasn't in the mood. Only two weeks had passed since Kramer's death. Carol sat quietly, waiting to see if Thorn would open up.

Pouring hot water for his tea, he finally spoke to her without looking up. "I meet with Welborne for lunch tomorrow about the bridge loan."

"Yes," she said, knowing it would be a key meeting. She was aware of the company's shaky financial condition and its need for capital. Kramer's death put the FCC approval on hold indefinitely. Consequently, Tachyon Communications, a large telecommunications firm, wanted to renegotiate its recent offer to buy stock in the company.

"It should be a formality," Thorn said. "You were at the board meeting when Welborne promised a $250,000 line of credit in case the deal with Tachyon was delayed."

Thorn looked over at Carol. She nodded, but her face indicated her mind was elsewhere. Thorn sympathized. She had her hands full with product development. He knew what that was like. The only possible training for such a job would be managing a rock band or coaching an NBA team. Her ability to get the developers to work together amazed him. He doubted that his having to deal with the rich, egotistical son of a senator was any more difficult.

"I'm sure he'll come through," she finally said, managing a slight smile in his direction. *At least he better,* she quietly reflected. *Or we're history.*

6

△ △ △

To succeed in the world, it is much more necessary to possess the penetration to discern who is a fool, than to discover who is a clever man.
—Charles-Maurice de Talleyrand,
Foreign Minister under Napoleon

KARL WALDRON, A.K.A. RAVEN, sat at the table in his dimly lit workroom at the Buenavista compound. As he rewound the tape he'd made of Thorn's conversation with Carol Jordan, a thin smile formed on his pale, pudgy face.

Raven had ordered phone taps and voice-activated bugs to be planted throughout Thorn's offices. When he heard the conversation between Thorn and Carol, he called Erica. He knew she would be pleased with him and enjoy the opportunity to listen to Thorn speak so innocently about the future of his company.

Erica looked up from the magazine she was reading to acknowledge Raven as he arrived at her spartan, highly organized workroom. By dyeing his hair jet black and avoiding the sun, he appeared much younger than his 45 years. No one would ever suspect that he had spent 21 of those years working for Stasi, the East German intelligence service, prior to the collapse of communism.

Raven cackled with glee. "He's getting desperate. With Kramer gone, he's got to kiss up to Welborne to get that loan, and you know he hates doing that."

Erica was less amused. "I think it's time you paid Welborne a visit."

"He'll be attending the monthly venture capital forum to-night at the University of Miami," said Raven. "He's on the panel, if you can believe it."

Erica allowed herself a hint of a smile. She knew the panel was supposed to be composed of business experts. Their role was to offer advice and criticism to a fledgling company that would be making a presentation for financing.

"You know what's happened to every company that followed his advice?" Raven asked, with a sarcastic leading tone.

"Out of business," she replied flatly.

"All except Thorn. He always agrees with Welborne, but ignores his advice. He knows he's useless," Raven said with some admiration. "To succeed in the world, it's much more important to identify the fool than discover a clever man."

Erica's glare reminded Raven that Thorn was the enemy. "That's why you're going to make sure Welborne doesn't give any more money to Thorn."

Raven stopped smiling.

* * * * *

Arriving late, Raven missed the presentation of the President of the biotech firm. He heard Welborne's final words, an inappropriate attempt at philosophy. "As the ancient Chinese proverb states, 'May you live in interesting times.'"

After the President answered questions from the audience, the formal meeting ended. The audience of entrepreneurs, lawyers, accountants and consultants began filing out, with some remaining to solicit business. Raven watched Welborne carefully, waiting to catch him where he could speak to him alone.

"Mr. Welborne," Raven said as he caught him on his way out of the auditorium, reaching out to shake his hand and introduce himself. "Larry Glover, Jensen Investments."

"Pleased to meet you," Welborne said, obviously used to such attention.

"I wanted to compliment you on your analysis. If they have any sense, they'll follow your advice," said Raven.

"Yes," said Welborne. "You know what they say, 'You can lead a horse to water but you cannot make him drink.'"

"You've been doing this for some time, I take it?" Raven asked.

"Yes, indeed," boasted Welborne. "I've been referred to as one of the pillars of the venture capital community here in South Florida."

Raven listened with feigned interest. "It must be hard on you to see a company fail from not following your advice."

Welborne nodded, adding a slight, compassionate shake of the head.

"What about companies you invest in?" Raven asked. "In those cases, it would be critical that they follow your advice."

"Well, most see the value of my guidance. It seldom becomes an issue," said Welborne.

"They would be wise to." Raven found that the more egotistical the mark, the easier it was to take him in. A brilliant person could easily be misled, so long as the ego was large enough.

"You know, I ran into someone a few months ago that mentioned you," Raven said. "I can't seem to place his name."

"Oh? I'm sure he had nothing good to say about me," said Welborne, laughing at his self-deprecating joke.

"That's what struck me as odd. He *didn't* have anything good to say about you. It surprised me, since your knowledge and experience are apparent."

"Who was it?" asked the thin-skinned Welborne.

"Like I said, I can't remember his name. He was in some kind of telecommunications business."

The puzzled look on Welborne's face surprised Raven. He had set up Welborne perfectly, but the fool still hadn't figured out who he was talking about. "Brown hair, slim build. I think he mentioned you were thinking of investing in his firm."

"Alec Thorn?"

"Yes. That's him." Raven held back his urge to smile.

"What was he saying about me?" demanded Welborne.

Putting on an air of compliance and objectivity, he replied, "The impression I got, sir, was he didn't want your help—that your advice would be useless."

Raven could see Welborne grow angry and wanted to make sure he stayed that way. "I certainly don't have your experience, Mr. Welborne, but it would seem to me that if an entrepreneur doesn't want your help, you should own at least 51% of the firm. This would ensure he followed your advice."

"Well, I'm a little surprised he would say that, but now that I think of it, he is a little rough around the edges. He might need a little horse breaking to get him used to the bit." Welborne took pride in his equestrian analogies, which he felt reflected well on his Palm Beach heritage.

"You're the expert, Mr. Welborne. This Thorn seemed a bit arrogant to me, like he knew better than everyone. I would hate to see you invest and have him make a fool of you."

"I am invested, dammit," said Welborne. "I've got $750 thousand into that company."

"You are?" asked Raven. "I'm sorry. I shouldn't have brought it up."

"No. No. I appreciate this information. It will influence my decision on the next round of financing. There's no way that I'll give him a cent unless I control the company," said Welborne.

Most of the crowd had left and Raven didn't want to linger, preferring instead to let Welborne stew overnight. "Do you have a card?"

Preoccupied with his thoughts, Welborne mechanically handed his card to Raven, who promised to call him the following week. Welborne walked away muttering to himself. Raven watched him leave and then laughed aloud, musing, *Give me 24 hours and I could convince that sap to run for President.*

7

There will be no end to the troubles of states, or of humanity itself, till philosophers become kings in this world, or till those we now call kings and rulers really and truly become philosophers, and political power and philosophy thus come into the same hands.

—Plato

RUNE CHAPMAN FROWNED as he heard his wife's shrill voice interrupt his meditation. "Honey, our appointment at Tiffany is in less than 30 minutes. The woman at the bridal registry is expecting us."

Chapman took a deep breath to dispel his annoyance. *She's bothering me to go shopping? At Tiffany?* Such a showy display of wealth always made him uneasy. He yelled to her from behind the closed door of his study, "You'll have to go alone."

Before he could continue, she flung open the door. "What? I can't hear you," she said as she entered the dimly lit room.

"I said, 'You'll have to go alone.' I have too much work to do."

"What work?" she asked. "You're just resting in your recliner. Come with me."

"I said I can't go," he snapped. Seeing her displeasure, he tried to soften his refusal. "Be sure to get them something nice, dear."

She knew further debate would be fruitless and sighed as she walked out, leaving the study door open.

Chapman waited until he heard the front door of their Fifth Avenue townhouse close before taking a deep breath. *What is it about women that makes them so concerned with shopping and trivialities? Is it hormonal? Don't they realize I have important things to do?*

He checked his watch and was relieved to see that he had 45 minutes before the Federal Open Market Committee would begin their meeting. The governors of the Federal Reserve would discuss whether to lower interest rates to stimulate the sluggish economy. Chapman wanted to ensure that they did not.

He walked past his large mahogany desk to shut the study door before he returned to his leather recliner. Taking a moment to admire the three walls full of his favorite books, many pre-medieval, Chapman sat glowing with pride, knowing he had the largest collection of incunabula in North America.

He relaxed with a few deep, measured breaths and then closed his eyes to meditate. Slowly, the room in which the committee held their meetings came into view. Chapman could not determine exactly how many people were at the meeting, but he could sense the presence of Peter Ryan, Chairman of the Federal Reserve and its most influential member.

Chapman had spent most of the week planting the thought in Ryan's mind that lowering interest rates would ignite disastrous inflation and that Ryan would be blamed for it. His term would last another two years, but no one on the committee, especially Ryan, wanted to see his name linked with economic ruin.

Word on the street was that the Fed would lower interest rates by ¼ to ½ percent to fuel the economy. The market had reacted to this news by bidding the price of Treasury securities and bonds higher. Chapman waited until prices reflected the street's sentiment and sold as many bonds as the market could bear through the countless investment funds that he controlled.

When the actual news that the Fed was not going to act reached the street, bond prices would drop and Chapman would repurchase the bonds he sold at a discount. Though his funds would earn millions of dollars, he would not personally profit from it. By forgoing such profits, he considered any actions that he took and any lies that he made in furtherance of his vision as justified.

Chapman allowed himself a broad smile. *Those arrogant, money-grubbing traders who think they're so smart. Don't they know that pride and greed are deadly sins? I'll just have to teach them a lesson.*

A decision by the Fed to postpone any action would deepen the economic slump and hurt the President's chances for reelection. Although Chapman had never met with him directly, the President had rejected Chapman's proposed economic and foreign policies. He was either ignorant or too arrogant to be enlightened. In either case, he needed to be disciplined. He, too, would either learn his lesson or someone more agreeable to Chapman would replace him.

Chapman had carefully studied the classic financial world battles between J.P. Morgan and President Roosevelt. *Morgan was an arrogant philistine,* thought Chapman. Back at the turn of the century, Morgan had publicly backed the President into a corner. *What did he expect him to do? Publicity is always bad.* Chapman gloated to himself, knowing his methods were much more subtle and effective.

Chapman returned his focus to the meeting. He sensed the overall mood favored lowering interest rates, but there were a number of uncommitted governors. They would seek Ryan's guidance. Chapman smiled. He had anticipated this scenario and wanted to get Ryan to announce his stance before the positions of the uncommitted governors hardened in favor of lowering rates.

He pictured himself inside of Ryan's head and began to resurface Ryan's fear of inflation. Ryan began to speak. The words were his own, but the thoughts that triggered them were Chapman's.

"I understand your concerns about the sluggish economy, but we must remember that not all regions of the country are equally affected by these conditions. Any decision we make should take into consideration the potential for increasing inflationary expectations. In short, we may be driving up costs and wages, which could bring even more harm to the economy."

Chapman smiled again. Ryan's speech would suffice. Now all he had to do was monitor the situation and make sure no one argued too strongly against the Chairman's caution. Towards the end of the debate, Chapman triggered Ryan again.

"Gentlemen," said Ryan. "I believe our best course of action is to postpone a decision for another six weeks. I move we revisit the issue at that time." Ryan's motion passed by a show of hands.

Chapman opened his eyes. He would have plenty of time to cover his positions. He pictured the talking heads on CNN and MSNBC trying to interpret the Fed's announcement and predict what would happen next. Even though he had helped establish the system, he was still amazed at how many people actually relied on these shows. The world was simple to Chapman—you just had to be at the top of the pyramid to see what was happening.

8

△ △ △

THORN LEFT HIS OFFICE just after noon to allow himself time to get to Welborne's Palm Beach country club. The opulent garden setting overlooking the golf course was where Welborne held most of his business meetings, mainly to impress entrepreneurs seeking capital. Thorn always enjoyed the setting, but would much rather have met back in Boca Raton and saved the 35 minutes spent driving. *At least I'll get a good meal,* Thorn thought, after having skipped breakfast to prepare for the meeting.

Thorn was not looking forward to his meeting but he knew that raising capital was an integral part of running a growth company. It was a small price to pay for not having to work for a large corporation.

Thorn smiled as he remembered his four-day career in corporate America 10 years earlier. On his first day, he was given a 350-page policy and procedures manual to read. The second day, he was reprimanded for bringing in a houseplant. The third day, they told him to take down the framed picture he hung in his cubicle.

They explained that employees at his E-level were not permitted a plant or a framed picture in their offices. If he had read the manual, he would have known that. He called in the fourth day to say he was sick—sick of having flaming assholes tell him what to do that had nothing to do with the company's business or his performance.

Thorn was still intolerant of bureaucracy, but he was learning how to deal with it. Just after forming his company, when an insurance agent told him he could reduce his premiums by adopting a board-approved policy and procedures manual, Thorn sat down and wrote one. Policy 1 was "Do everything you say you're going to do." Policy 2 was "Don't do anything you wouldn't want to see on the evening news." Those two rules, as far as he was concerned, would satisfactorily cover the company's policies. Welborne had argued at a board meeting that they should create the image of a big company and put together a comprehensive manual. Thorn offered to create a task force to explore the issue. In the meantime, he argued they should approve this manual and start saving money. As Thorn expected, Welborne forgot about the task force.

Thorn arrived at the club restaurant and was ushered back to Welborne's table, where he was entertaining the waitress with his tales of fox hunting in England. Fresh off the golf course, Welborne wore a fancy white golf cap and polo shirt, both embroidered with the crest of the old-line club.

Thorn waited for Welborne to finish his story and the waitress to express her admiration. He had heard this story several times already.

"Hello, Martin. It's good to see you," Thorn said, shaking hands with Welborne.

"Hello, Alec. Sit down," said Welborne quietly.

"Have you invited that beautiful young lass to your next outing?" asked Thorn.

Welborne ignored Thorn's comment, which surprised him. He knew the tall, dark-haired Welborne regarded his prowess with women as another of his great assets. "I'll be meeting some foreign dignitaries shortly, so I won't be having lunch. Feel free, however, to order something if you'd like," Welborne said patronizingly.

"No thanks, Martin. As it turns out, I ate a late breakfast," Thorn lied.

Both Thorn and Welborne ordered iced tea from the waitress when she returned. Thorn could see that Welborne was not in his normal expansive mood.

"You know Alec," Welborne said, "the company is not doing well and I'm a little disturbed."

Thorn waited for Welborne to finish venting. After that, he'd take the paperwork for the line of credit from his jacket pocket and close the deal.

"What I'm most upset over is that you didn't put any of my money away for a rainy day. You just continued on blithely, without regard for the company's future."

Thorn knew this was a gross misrepresentation, but still he waited.

"If you had listened to me, the company wouldn't be in this mess," Welborne said.

"It's my recollection that everyone agreed to the plan at the last board meeting," Thorn said. "Company expenditures are exactly in line with the budget that you approved. The only variation is that Kramer died and the FCC approval has been delayed. If he were still alive, we'd be celebrating a $10 million, multi-year contract right now."

Welborne appeared distracted and was not listening to Thorn. "You see, Alec, what you needed was a little Kentucky windage in your budget. You shouldn't have bet the farm on a single contract."

"We didn't bet the farm on a single contract, Martin." Thorn's exasperation was barely concealed by his tone of voice. "Two corporations are still interested in buying stock. I didn't push them because I knew our bargaining position would dramatically improve upon our getting FCC approval. At first, they were only talking $2.50 a share. Tachyon's offer went up to $7 a share when they thought we might get the approval this quickly. With the contract in hand, we could have gotten $10 a share, and we wouldn't even need their money."

"What about sales?" Welborne immediately asked. "I told you we needed a VP of Sales and Marketing. If you had hired a sales professional, you wouldn't be in this mess, either."

"We already *discussed* this," Thorn said, his voice rising. He shifted his body forward, so that he was now sitting on the front edge of his chair. "Two weeks ago, we were on the verge of having more business than we could handle, Martin." He slowed his pace and drew in a breath, letting it out slowly. "We still have numerous contracts pending. When word leaked out that the FCC was evaluating our high-speed wireless application, everyone decided to wait and see what happened. It wouldn't matter if we had 10 salespeople in the field."

Thorn kept his voice steady, but inwardly he seethed. He did not want to point out that he had based his strategy on Welborne acting rationally. Offering the line of credit was prudent for both Welborne and the company. Thorn expected Welborne to ask for some stock options to sweeten the deal and he was prepared to give him some. This surprise attack was, to Thorn, both outrageous and unjustified.

Welborne owned a third of the company. Thorn knew it was unwise to anger a large shareholder, if it could be avoided. He remembered his lawyer's explanation of the "golden rule" of investing, "He who has the gold makes the rules." Still, it didn't make it right. Thorn committed himself to biting the bullet, at least for the moment.

Welborne said, "You failed and I think you should own up to it."

Thorn gritted his teeth. One more idiotic comment like that and he would plainly tell Welborne what he thought of him and his expertise. "I thought I came here to discuss the terms of the line of credit that you promised at the board meeting," Thorn said. "What is it that you want?"

"Line of credit? With the company in a shambles, you think anyone will give you a line of credit?"

Thorn refused to dignify Welborne's outburst with a response.

"The only way I can ensure this company is run properly is to make sure I have control," Welborne said.

Thorn was resigned to the fact that he would not reach a deal with Welborne. He waited to hear Welborne's offer before dismissing it. "What are you offering?"

"I am willing to put up the $250,000 at $0.50 per share," said Welborne.

"That's less than you paid a year ago when we were just starting out!" yelled Thorn. Obviously, Welborne had done the math to see what price would be required to gain majority control. "I could understand $2.50 per share based on the offers of the two corporate investors, but fifty cents is ridiculous!"

Thorn left unsaid his thought that he would rather shut down his company than sell Welborne control of it at that price.

Welborne's smugness disappeared. He was surprised Thorn did not cave in to his demands, but he figured he still held the upper hand. "You're not going to make a fool out of me," he said.

Thorn was taken aback by Welborne's non sequitur. *What did 'make a fool out of me' have to do with anything?* It was a perfect opening for Thorn to attack. "You don't need me," Thorn said before hesitating. He was going to finish his sentence with "to make a fool out of you." Instead, he said, "to kick around." The sharper barb was justified, but it would have earned Welborne's eternal hatred.

Thorn rose and looked at Welborne. "Thanks for the iced tea," Thorn said as he left.

9

△ △ △

Speech was given to man to conceal his thoughts.
—Charles-Maurice de Talleyrand
Foreign Minister under Napoleon

THE HOT FLORIDA SUN beat down upon the Buenavista compound, but with the blinds drawn and the air conditioner churning away, Raven was oblivious to the outdoor heat. Eyes closed, deep in trance, he clutched Welborne's business card in his hand. Slowly, Raven opened his eyes and a knowing smile began to form on his lips. *This is good, very good,* he reflected, knowing he had to tell Erica right away. Getting up and going over to his desk, he called her cell phone.

"Yes," she answered.

"Are you available?" he asked.

"Yes."

"I'll have to call you back," he said and hung up. Both recognized that this was not the type of information that they could discuss over the telephone, especially a cell phone. It required a more confidential means of communication.

He closed his eyes again and pictured her face. He waited until she had a good mental lock on him and then thought, *"The meeting's over. They won't be working together."*

"How sure are you?"

"I could feel the hatred building between them. I kept repeating to Welborne 'He's making a fool of you.' Thorn was ready to physically attack him."

"You're sure he won't give him any money?" she asked.

29

"*Positive. I'll give Welborne a call and make sure, though,*" he thought.

"*Good,*" she thought and, smiling at the outcome, broke contact.

* * * * *

Thorn chose to take the scenic route down A1A on his drive back to the office, not wanting anyone to see him when he was in a bad mood. Besides, the views of the ocean and the Intracoastal Waterway often would lift his spirits.

Thorn reflected on Welborne's performance at the meeting. His anger seemed contrived. Welborne could be difficult, but this was ridiculous. Thorn wondered if he was too harsh in his words to Welborne. No, he knew that wasn't true. Welborne *needed* to have his plan shot down immediately. Better to nip the problem in the bud than to lead him to think it was a reasonable offer.

Thorn thought again of Welborne's comment about "making a fool out of him." *Sure Welborne acts like a fool, at least some of the time, but he did come up with the money to turn my dream into reality. He had bought into my vision in the beginning, and I certainly hope his investment pays off. I'm working hard to make it happen, but to cede control to Welborne would let down the employees and ruin the company. That is not going to happen.*

When Thorn got back to the office, he would fire up talks with the two corporations that had expressed interest earlier. He knew he had barely a month before they would be out of money. Since there really *was* no Kentucky windage in the budget, the only way he could see to postpone the company's extinction would be to lay off people. But he *hated* to do this—Thorn knew his employees were his most valuable assets. *Those corporate titans who downsize companies to make them more profitable are shortsighted assholes. They're throwing out thousands of man-years of expertise just to increase the value of their stock options. This is not good management. It's criminal.*

Thorn's digression did not solve his problem. He needed money—fast.

10

△△△

HEADING SOUTH ON A1A, Thorn decided to postpone his return to the office and stop at Mizner Park in downtown Boca Raton. He knew that he always felt good walking around the beautifully land-scaped mall and that he could get a tasty meal at one of the outdoor cafes there. *Some grilled dolphin would hit the spot,* he thought.

Thorn valet parked his seven-year old silver Honda Accord at Max's Grill, a trendy nouveau cuisine restaurant. As Thorn handed the yuppie-looking attendant his keys, he ignored the younger man's sneer, which obviously derived from his preference toward parking Porsches and Mercedes.

He strolled past a few of the fancy shops featuring leather and other exotic fashions. A store with glass figurines caught his eye. He peered into the window when he noticed a woman approach-ing him in the reflection. Turning around, he found himself star-ing into the clear green eyes of the florist from the previous day.

"What are you doing here?" he asked. "Don't you have a shop to run?"

"I'm glad we ran into each other," she said, ignoring his question.

"How did you find me? I didn't know where I was going until the last minute."

She laughed. "Did I find you or did you find me?"

Thorn hesitated. "Are you saying I was looking for you?"

"I let you know I had something to tell you and where I'd be. Your intuition did the rest," she said.

"Why didn't you just call me?"

31

"I don't have your number," she replied. "Besides, I don't like to talk over the phone—you never know who might be listening."

Thorn laughed. "Look, here's my business card. I'll write my cell phone number on the back." He handed her the card. *I don't even know her name,* he thought.

"Sophie Kyros," she said and handed him the card to her floral shop.

Thorn hesitated, wondering how she knew what he was thinking. He shook his head and dismissed the thought, figuring it would be natural for someone to introduce herself when exchanging business cards. "What is it you wanted to tell me?"

"You met the man with the hat, right?"

Thorn flinched as he remembered that Welborne had been wearing a golf cap. "Yes."

"Well, they're upset that you're putting up such a fight. They may try something more desperate and I want us to be ready."

"Who? Ready for what?" he asked, obviously flustered. "Welborne works alone. He's too lazy to do something desperate," Thorn argued.

"Not him. He's just a pawn," she said, a more graven expression appearing on her face. "Your real enemies are going to reveal themselves very soon."

11

△ △ △

The surest way to remain poor is to be an honest man.
—Napoleon Bonaparte

HAWKE SAT AT THE kitchen table waiting for the "boss lady" to return, occupying himself by disassembling, cleaning and reassembling his collection of handguns. He looked up as Erica entered. "Everything is in place. I can set it off with a telephone call from anywhere in the world." Hawke smiled with pride. "In fact, it *will* go off, if I don't call to disarm it every 48 hours."

"No trouble?" she asked, reminded of his difficulties with the Russians.

"No," he replied, somewhat defensively. "What about our buyer?" he asked, quickly shifting the focus away from himself. "Did Raven's man come through?"

"There's been a change in plan."

He waited for her to continue, his interest piqued. He hated Raven.

"Use the PN14 line to call Baghdad. Notify Saddam that we have a nuclear device for sale."

"That line's monitored. NATO will know what we're up to before Saddam."

"Exactly," she said. "Let them know we're also talking to North Korea. They've been in the market for some time."

A hint of a smile grew on Hawke's face. Erica could see he understood and waited for him to speak.

"There's no need to sell it to terrorists," he said, thinking out loud. His smile grew broader. "We'll use NATO's money to buy influence in countries around the world."

Erica smiled. "Dictators are a lot cheaper, nowadays, thanks to the collapse of the Soviet Union."

I will never be humiliated again, she vowed.

12

△ △ △

Never trouble another for what you can do for yourself.
—Thomas Jefferson

THORN WOKE UP before his alarm went off with an unusual sense of calmness. Laying there in the dark, he stared at the illuminated LED clock—5:45—and sensed peacefulness within himself, even though in less than two weeks, he had gone from being poised on top of the world to running a company without any money. Rolling out of bed, he spied the oil on his dresser, given to him by the eccentric florist. He had followed her instructions carefully, not fully knowing why, and reflected back on her words—she had predicted that a man with a hat would offer a bad deal to him. That was Welborne. What else did she say? Take vitamins. He laughed, realizing he'd missed both breakfast and lunch the day before. Thorn went to his closet to take out the multi-vitamins. Her advice had been sound and the three days would be up the following day. *Yes,* he decided, *I'll visit her again.*

At the office, Thorn followed up with investors who had expressed interest in his company earlier in the month. He knew he had to walk a fine line between pushing for immediate consideration and appearing anxious. Thorn was fully aware that savvy investors could smell fear a mile away and traditionally avoid such opportunities like the plague, no matter how lucrative they might appear.

Carol came into his office to check in with him, sensing that he might need a little cheering up or at least a friendly ear. "I asked my brother up in New York if he could help," she said. "He told

35

me there are quite a few investment bankers in his building, but the ones he knows are all bond traders. His insurance company can't invest in anything this small, either."

Thorn smiled, genuinely appreciating her caring actions. "I would have guessed that, but thanks for making the effort."

"Any luck with the other investors?" she asked.

"Johnson at Tachyon is boating in Michigan for two weeks. I can't go around him and speak to anyone else without his permission. That would be political suicide." She noted that his demeanor and tone of voice hadn't gone down or become depressive as he spoke about the delay, and wondered to herself what was responsible for his newfound ease.

Thorn continued, "Our contact at AK Wireless Systems told me that they're reorganizing to 'proactively reengineer their core processes and create a new paradigm of empowered team dynamics.'"

"What does that mean?" she asked, baffled by the corporate-speak.

"They have no idea what they're doing and are hoping that no one notices," Thorn answered. "It will be at least six months before they can recover from their reorganization and get back to business." Again, he seemed undaunted.

"What about the FCC approval?" she probed, going through all their options.

"Everyone is still in shock at Kramer's death. They're not going to do anything until his position is filled, which could take some time. We're going to have to find another advocate to push this through."

"Have you talked to any of the employees here?"

"No. You're the only one who knows what's happening. I'd like to have a solution before I disclose a major problem."

"Do you think they might be willing to defer their salaries or reduce them for awhile?" she wondered aloud.

He gazed at her a moment, feeling grateful for how she was thinking things through with him. "You mean in return for more stock options? I thought about that, Carol, but they're already getting stock options. If this company flies, they'll all make out. They won't give up cash for more stock," Thorn reasoned.

"The only way we'll know for sure is to ask them, Alec."

"You think they'd go for it?"

"If you explain that other investors are interested, but there's a timing problem, I think so."

"You *really* think they'd do it?" he asked again, skeptical but hoping she was right.

Carol faced him directly, looking her boss squarely in the eye. "I think you underestimate the loyalty you've built up with the employees. They know you sold your house to start this company, Alec, and that you've worked without a salary for over a year." Her admiration was apparent, and she saw there really was no argument in his eyes. "If you asked them to sacrifice, I think they'd do it."

Thorn's eyes met her gaze in kind. *What's she feeling right now?* he wondered. Instantly, he caught himself and refocused his attention to the business at hand. "Okay, you're on," he said with a smile. "Call a meeting for this afternoon. We'll find out what they're willing to do."

Carol paused a moment before turning around and heading back down the hall to her office. *Well, he seemed unusually buoyant for not having any idea in hell where the next dollar's coming from. What's up with that?* Simultaneously, she felt a subtle welling up of affection for Mr. Alec Thorn, her boss, and she wasn't quite sure what to make of that, either.

13

△△△

The world is governed by very different personages from what is imagined by those who are not behind the scenes.
—Benjamin Disraeli

CHAPMAN HEARD THE ring of his private line. He rose from his recliner and walked to his desk as quickly as his 62-year-old legs would take him. Only six people had this number.

"Yes," he answered.

"It's me."

Chapman recognized Hawke's voice. Knowing Hawke would be calling from a pay phone, he checked to ensure the line was secure. "Go ahead."

"She decided to try to get NATO to pay. I'm going to notify the others that there'll be an auction, but it's just for show."

"I understand. Anything else?"

"No."

Chapman envisioned Hawke standing at a street corner pay phone. He reflected on how effective he'd been recently, as part of the unfolding plan. "Very well. Keep me informed."

Pleased with the news, Chapman hung up the phone and returned to his recliner. *Erica was never properly educated,* he mused, *but she learned quickly. Certainly, selling nuclear weapons to terrorists is profitable. The only drawback is the lack of follow-on business. Once they have a nuke, they don't need lots of other weapons.* He laughed wryly to himself. *What's worse, they might decide to use it. After all, terrorists are often a rather unstable lot.*

He wondered if she had considered the idea of extorting NATO *before* he planted the idea in her head. The ring of his private line interrupted him. "Yes," he answered.

"Are we still on schedule?" asked a voice with a distinctly upper-class English accent. "Is she, as it were, under control?"

"I'll handle her. Just see to it that your envoy takes a hard line, but okays payment."

"What about your end?"

"He'll do what he's told. If not, we'll leak the fact they succumbed to extortion."

"Ta-ta."

Chapman smiled as he hung up. *The arrogant President needs a lesson in humility, while Erica needs guidance. She has great leadership potential, like many Presidents, Prime Ministers and kings.* He paused and then laughed confidently. *I've handled them—I'll handle her, as well.*

14

△ △ △

Don't fight a battle if you don't gain anything by winning.
—Erwin Rommel, Nazi General

ERICA AND RAVEN SAT around her worktable listening to Thorn's conversation with Carol Jordan. Neither of them was smiling.

"He still needs money," said Raven, barely a second after their conversation ended. "Even if the employees agree to wage reductions. I can make sure the corporate investors don't come through."

"That's not the problem," she replied. "Welborne is going to crack."

"Why do you say that? In his mind, Welborne is convinced that Thorn is playing him for a fool. He won't change his mind."

"No," she responded bluntly. "Welborne wants to be liked. Once he finds out the employees are with Thorn, he'll fold." Erica looked at Raven with a sense of certainty.

"Why? He just has to stand his ground. He's not obligated to invest in Thorn's company."

"He's not like most people," she quickly responded. "He's never faced adversity *in his life*. He's the kid on the block who took his ball home when he didn't get his way." Her mocking facial expression matched her tone of voice. "And when he finds out they have another ball to play with, he'll come back with all sorts of equipment."

Erica stared into the distance, unfocused and silent, trying to visualize the outcome in her own mind. "He's going to justify it in his mind by saying that only by constructive engagement, or some such diplomatic mumbo-jumbo, can he maintain his influence."

"He has no influence."

"He'll never admit that," she retorted. "No. We need to put Thorn on the sidelines. He's too close."

Walking over to her desk, she pressed the intercom to call Hawke. "I need you here."

She looked at Raven, who could not hide his displeasure, nor his hatred for Hawke. To have him take over a project that he was overseeing enraged him. Erica didn't care, knowing Hawke hated Raven equally. She needed them both, but she encouraged their mutual hatred. There was no danger of a coup, as long as the two underlings remained divided. Erica's intuitive feel for balance of power politics was superb.

A knock on the door signaled Hawke had arrived. "Come in," she said.

Erica pointed to a chair, where Hawke joined them. "I need Thorn to have an accident." She paused and looked sternly into his eyes. "But I *don't* want him killed."

"Why fight a battle if you don't gain anything by winning?" Hawke asked, annoyed with this distraction. "He doesn't even know who we are."

"He will," she replied calmly.

"How?"

"Because I'm going to tell him—that's how. I want him to know. I want him to remember what he *did* to me. I want him to see everything and to know that this time he won't stop me," she said, her voice rising.

The veins in Hawke's face stood out. "That's crazy. He's never even met you. Why risk years of work just because of some weird dreams that you've had. If you think he's a risk, let's just kill him."

"Shut up!" she yelled, standing up out of her chair and piercing him with a penetrating stare. "I'm giving the orders around here! When I found you, you were nothing but a two-bit mercenary fighting useless wars in Africa and working for half-cocked drug lords! *I'm* the one who pulled you out of there and put several million dollars in your pocket! Don't forget it! If you want out of this operation, then get out! If not, then *shut up* and do what you're told!"

Hawke turned his eyes to the floor, got up from his chair, and left without a word.

15

△ △ △

The strength of a wall is neither greater nor less than the courage of the men who defend it.
—Genghis Khan

BOBBY HUNTER AND the six members of his handpicked anti-terrorist team waited for night to fall outside the gated walls of Miguel Rojas' hacienda outside Cali, Colombia. Security was tight, there, even by drug lord standards. Inside the electrified walls, armed guards roamed like army ants, while the entire compound was safeguarded with video surveillance cameras, infrared light beams, motion and heat detectors, pressure sensors, trip wires and attack dogs. Still, Hunter was not concerned, knowing beyond a shadow of a doubt that each of his men was fearless and extraordinarily well trained. *The goons guarding this fortress will undoubtedly fold,* he reasoned.

Hunter needed to take Rojas alive, knowing the drug lord could tell him the whereabouts of Hawke, the man who'd designed the elaborate security system. Hunter would let his team members split the $1 million bounty placed on Rojas' head by the Colombian government and the United States DEA. For them, it was a job. For Hunter, it was payback time.

16

△ △ △

THORN ENTERED THE florist shop and was immediately met by Sophie. "I've been waiting for you," she said. "I have to leave in a few minutes. I was hoping you'd come early."

Checking his watch, he saw he'd arrived 20 minutes early.

"Good. You brought the water," she said, gently taking the vase from him. "You have the oil?"

"Yes," he replied, reaching into his pocket and handing it to her.

"Wait here. I'll be right back." Sophie disappeared into the back of her shop, and a minute later, reappeared with the oil. Handing it to him, she instructed him, "Keep using it every night before bed."

"What's in this?" Thorn asked, his face showing more than a little curiosity.

"Lots of things. Herbs, spices—some good, some bad," she replied, grinning impishly.

"Bad things?"

"Yes," she said with a laugh, "but they're good, overall. They'll build up your resistance to the negative that surrounds you."

"You mean like a vaccination?"

"Yes, but it works on a spiritual level."

Thorn was not sure what to make of her explanation.

"I have to go, now," she said. "Come back on Saturday. And call me when you dream of water."

With that, she began the process of locking up her florist shop. Standing at the doorway for a moment, Thorn looked back at this perky, little woman, realizing she'd been right on the money about everything up to that moment. He wondered, though, just how she could predict he'd be having a specific kind of *dream.*

17

△ △ △

HUNTER ENTERED THE back of the truck carrying a briefcase. Inside, Rojas sat gagged and bound to a chair. A quick nod from Hunter sent the man guarding Rojas out the back door, leaving Hunter alone with the drug lord.

Slowly, Hunter peeled off the black mask that had concealed his face during the raid. He relished, like a jackal nearing his helpless prey, the look of horror in Rojas' eyes. To him, Hunter was "El Diablo," the scourge of Colombia, a man whose brutality surpassed that of the old Medellin cartel.

Hunter put his briefcase on the table next to Rojas, opening it so that Rojas could not see the contents, knowing the added uncertainty would increase his fear. He took his time, alternately looking into his briefcase and at Rojas, as if the man's face would determine what instrument of torture to select.

Reaching in, Hunter silently turned on a tape recorder and elected to use a scalpel. He held it up to the light to check the blade for sharpness, leaving Rojas to wonder how he might decide to use it. Standing next to him, he drew the scalpel closer to Rojas, holding it, with surgeon-like precision, next to his throat. Rojas closed his eyes.

With a quick flick, Hunter slit the gag in Rojas' mouth and pulled it free. Rojas opened his eyes, aware he wasn't dead. "Whatever you want, it's yours! Money, drugs, distributors . . . I can get you anything! Mother of God, please don't kill me!" Rojas gasped to catch his breath.

Hunter had always counted on his carefully constructed identity as El Diablo and its shock value to get his answers as quickly as possible. As far as both this drug lord and the DEA were concerned, El Diablo was a vicious drug dealer taking over the operations of the now defunct Medellin cartel. There was only one man in Latin America, the CIA station chief in Colombia, who knew his true identity; unfortunately, he was now dead, thanks to Hawke, who also fabricated the evidence pointing to El Diablo as the killer.

"There's a safe in the bedroom, under the carpet," said Rojas. "At least $5 million in cash. A complete list of *Federales* on my payroll. I can give you the combination."

Hunter decided Rojas had revealed enough information to be of value to the *Federales* and held up his hand indicating that Rojas should shut up, which he did. Hunter turned off the tape recorder. "Where is Hawke?"

Rojas' eyes again betrayed his fear, as he hesitated, wondering whether it would be better to die at the hand of El Diablo or risk Hawke returning to inflict an even more painful death.

He paused for only a moment, before electing to postpone his death a little longer. "He's not here."

Hunter glared fiercely at Rojas, making it clear that if he had to pull the information out of him, it would be painful. "He hasn't been here for weeks. Once security was in place, he got paid and left. He told me you were dead."

Hunter had no need for words. He reached back into his briefcase and removed another scalpel, this one with a curved tip.

"He's in Florida," Rojas quickly volunteered.

"Where in Florida?" Hunter demanded. He had a good idea, but hoped that Rojas could save him time by confirming it.

"I have a number to call . . . 561-392-2500."

Hunter memorized the number without writing it down. *Probably an answering service, but the 561 area code includes Boca Raton.* Hunter felt certain he'd find him.

18

△ △ △

THORN LAY IN BED, neither awake nor asleep, but rather in that in-between state of consciousness. He dreamt he was on an Alaskan cruise and all around him were snow-capped mountains. Though just beyond his remembrance, he knew a raging storm had come and gone and now, the sun was shining brightly overhead.

Thorn slowly drifted into full consciousness. He pondered the significance of his dream. *Why a cruise? I've never really liked the idea of being bottled up on a ship surrounded by water. And what about the storm? I felt no fear, though I sensed it had been intense. Was that important?*

Putting his dream-reflections on hold, he began readying himself for a meeting he'd scheduled with his lawyer.

* * * * *

Chapman was expecting Hawke's call at 9. At 8:59 the phone rang.

"Yes."

"It's me."

"Go on."

"She's acting weird."

"In what way?" Chapman sounded irritated—he didn't have time for chitchat.

"She wants me to make sure some small business owner has an accident."

"What?!"

"I know. It doesn't make sense. She's hell bent on screwing up some guy that owns a small telecommunication business."

"Is this something new?" Chapman asked.

"No," Hawke replied. "I didn't bother to mention it before, because I figured she was on the rag."

He winced at the mercenary's language, but he knew what Hawke meant. *With all those hormones flowing through their bodies, most women are unstable,* he thought, *but it's not like Erica to act irrationally.*

"Who is this guy?"

"Alec Thorn. He lives in an apartment on the beach in Boca Raton."

"Is he in the business?"

"No. I checked him out. He's clean."

"Anything else?"

"No."

Chapman hung up, having got what he needed from Hawke. Clearly, he would have to investigate this Thorn.

* * * * *

Traffic was moderate, as Thorn traveled south on I-95 to Ft. Lauderdale. Since he'd heard from Carol that his employees had agreed to defer their salaries for one month in return for stock options, Thorn knew that the first thing he needed to do upon arriving at the office was to talk to his lawyer about the paperwork.

He was running late and pushing his Honda beyond the unofficial left lane speed limit of 80. Suddenly, his car's engine stopped running, going silent, stone-cold dead.

Though the steering worked fine, with no power, Thorn knew he had to cross over three lanes quickly to get to the side of the road. Waiting for a large semi-trailer to pass, he avoided using his brakes since any speed lost while braking would only increase the likelihood of an accident.

Concentrating on his rearview and side mirrors, he didn't notice the paint bubbling on the front hood. The truck passed and, miraculously, traffic parted briefly in the next two lanes, enabling him to get over easily. Seeing the exit for Cypress Creek coming up, Thorn headed for the turn-off and slowly pressed on the brakes, now noticing bright orange flames licking out from under the hood. Thorn steered the car off the exit ramp and onto a nearby grass infield. He swung the door open and jumped out of the car as soon as he came to a stop.

Thorn walked away from the car until he felt he was a safe distance away. Stopping 30 feet away, he watched as the entire car became engulfed in flames. The black smoke spewing from the wreck got thicker when the tires caught fire. He couldn't help but wonder what this meant, as he walked down the block to a nearby gas station to call his lawyer.

"John," he said, "I'm going to be late for our meeting. But I have a good excuse."

"You always have a good excuse," his lawyer said. "What is it this time?"

"My car blew up," said Thorn.

John Brewer laughed. "Well, at least you weren't in it."

"No. I *was* in it," Thorn replied. "You might even see it on the news tonight."

Brewer stopped laughing. "You're not hurt, are you?"

"No," he said, pausing to think over what he had to do next. "Damn! I'm going to have to wait until the fire's out, get this thing towed, fill out accident forms and rent a car. This is going to waste half my day!"

"You're alive and unhurt, Alec," Brewer said, trying to provide some perspective.

"Yeah." He added sarcastically, "Great, huh?"

* * * * *

Indeed, the local tabloid news station showed footage of the car billowing smoke on the five o'clock news. Erica smiled, until the newscaster reported that no one was hurt in the fire. Though his name was not mentioned, she knew it was Thorn and that he'd escaped her attempt to sideline him. Erica picked up the phone and called Hawke. "Get over here!" she screamed.

Minutes later, he knocked at her door.

Swinging the door open, she demanded, "What happened?" her face filled with rage.

"It doesn't make any sense," he said, walking in and shaking his head. "He should be in the hospital covered with burns—but somehow, he walked away without a scratch."

His down turned eyes and slightly red face displayed his embarrassment. An expert in demolitions, Hawke knew very well how to start all kinds of fires. "Something unusual is going on here," he said.

"Okay," she replied, still full of anger. "Let's stop screwing around. Kill him!"

19

△△△

Enlighten people generally, and tyranny and oppressions of body and mind will vanish like evil spirits at the dawn of day.

—Thomas Jefferson

"COME WITH ME," Sophie said, leading Thorn into the back of her shop.

She gestured to a chair and invited Thorn to sit.

"You're not hurt, are you?" she asked.

"No. I'm fine," he said, squinting slightly at her. "You knew about my accident?"

"Yes," she said. "You're lucky you came to me when you did."

"You mean it would have been worse?" asked Thorn, visualizing what might have happened.

"After I saw you on Thursday, I prayed all night that you'd be okay," she said, her eyes turning compassionately toward Thorn. He felt a soft, calming energy emanating from her as she stood next to him. "I actually cried seeing what they were trying to do to you."

"Who are *they*?" Thorn asked, staring up into Sophie's eyes. "Why would anyone want to hurt me? I'm a nobody." He looked at her hoping for an answer. "I don't have anything that anyone would want. I don't understand."

"You will very soon," she said, handing him a pale blue oval stone.

"What's this?" he asked. "An eyeball?"

"It's a third eye. It will help you to identify your enemies."

"A what?"

"A third eye," she said. "It will help me to open one of your chakras."

"Chakras? Isn't that some kind of Indian-Hindu thing?"

"They're energy transformers. Everyone has them." She paused. "Yours are mostly closed." Her face registered no judgment or humor.

"Is that bad?"

"Only a glimmer of the spiritual energy available to you is getting through. But it's not surprising," she said. "You closed your chakras in a defensive reaction to all the envy and hatred that they heaped on top of you."

"I closed them?"

"Not consciously. It was instinctive. Your natural tendency is to pick up on the pain of others and take it upon yourself. They knew this and used it against you."

"I'm not like that at all," Thorn argued. "I always make logical decisions, especially in business. I don't let my emotions get in the way."

She smiled. "Consciously, you *are* very logical. But your heart and your mind do not act as one. You try to hide your compassion. But it's obvious to those that can see."

"If that's true, shouldn't I try to get rid of this hatred that you say is responsible?"

"That's what I did," she said.

Thorn stopped for a moment to consider her answer. Instantly, elements of the dream he'd had appeared in his mind. As the tour boat was being guided through a violent storm, waves crashed over the ship forcing everyone below; yet he had remained on top letting the water wash over him. When the storm subsided, he could see glaciers and beautiful snow-capped mountains, but he also saw that the ocean water had turned a murky brown. A sense of understanding came over Thorn as he looked over at her, meeting her knowing gaze. "You baptized me," he whispered.

She nodded, then rose to announce that their meeting was over. Thorn followed her to the door.

"You may feel some discomfort in the next day or so while I work on you," she said.

"Headaches? Pins and needles-type sensations?"

She nodded. "I know you already feel it, but it may get worse, like a muscle that gets sore when you overdo it. Just remember, it's for a good cause." She smiled.

"Obviously, you know what you're doing," Thorn said. "Can you teach me how to do this?"

She laughed as she opened the door.

"Are you making fun of me?" he asked.

"No," she replied, halting her laughter, but maintaining a broad smile.

"Are you saying that this is a skill you can't teach? You either have it or you don't?"

"No. Anyone can learn how to do this."

"Then why is it so funny?"

"You already know how," she answered.

"I can't do what you do."

"That's because you've forgotten. When I'm finished, you'll remember. Everything will fall into place."

"You're sure?"

She smiled confidently and nodded her head. "I'm sure.

20

△△△

Knowledge is power.

—Francis Bacon

GECKO ANSWERED HIS phone at the Pentagon in his usual brusque manner, "What?"

"Excuse me sir, but something came up and I was hoping that I might bring it to your attention."

He recognized White's voice. The young NSA analyst had used the code phrase indicating he wanted to meet, rather than speak over the telephone.

"Call me later," said Gecko, signaling him he'd be able to meet him shortly at their typical rendezvous.

His closest associates in Washington knew George K. Olsen, United States Department of Defense Special Coordinator for Intelligence and Planning, as "Gecko." Having risen through the ranks over two decades and numerous administrations, his fancy title granted him access to the highest levels of intelligence. Not that he hadn't earned it. His forte was resolving foreign crises in ways that could never be traced to the administration. No one in the Defense Department quite understood how he managed to accomplish such works and no one asked. All they knew was that he produced results. Though he reported to the Secretary of Defense, most insiders knew his influence was far greater. They also knew not to annoy him—those who had, consistently found themselves without jobs.

Gecko was not impressed with the ineffectual White. He had arranged for his employment at the NSA over two years earlier and

White had yet to bring him any information of value. He even had considered having him fired, so he could eliminate the quarterly cash stipend White was paid over and above his official pay. As he put on his jacket, he made a mental note—if White was wasting his time, he was off the payroll.

* * * * *

Gecko left his office and walked down the block, stopping into a nearby Starbucks, where he saw White sitting at a table near the back wall. While ordering a coffee, he subtly surveyed the place, scanning for anyone that might recognize him. Picking up his coffee, he moved to the back table and sat down across from White. "What do you have for me?"

"Someone used an unsecured line to contact the Iraqi Presidential Complex. The man on the phone said, 'They have a package for sale and are asking $3 billion.' Seemed to be an American male, aged 35 to 40 years old. No regional accent detectable."

"Do we know where it originated?"

"A pay phone in Boca Raton, Florida. They used a prepaid phone card to piggyback on an old CIA line, left over from the days when we supported Saddam."

"Any response?"

"They're going to call back with more details."

"All right, go ahead and notify your supervisor."

"Of course, sir. That's what I intended."

"Keep me informed," Gecko said, as he stood up and looked around the room once more.

White stood up. "Sit down," said Gecko. "You can leave after you finish your coffee."

21

△ △ △

HUNTER SAT MAKING small talk with a plain-looking divorcée at the end of the second bar at Gigi's Tavern, an upscale oyster bar in Mizner Park, the type of meat market Hunter knew Hawke would frequent. He knew it was a long shot, but so long as the women kept coming, he'd sit tight.

Hunter had met Hawke only once, but had a good understanding of his profile: he wouldn't have a girlfriend, but would prefer to pick up female company whenever he felt the urge. Being a loner, a steady girlfriend would be a burden that could be used against him. Like any good mercenary, he wanted nothing that would complicate his life, a life that could force him to leave town at a moment's notice and assume a new identity for months at a time. He formed no allegiances, simply going where the money was best.

Hunter watched as more women entered the bar, *a parade of grand proportion,* he thought to himself. He continued scanning the restaurant, studying the women. Some young ones stood out, but most were between the ages of 30 to 45. On the whole, they were above average in appearance, wore expensive jewelry and took great pains to make themselves attractive. They would be the type Hawke would choose. Recently divorced, possibly discarded by their ex-husbands in favor of young hardbodies, they would be easily seduced by Hawke's tall, lithe physique and international flair.

The woman sitting next to him bored him silly, but he was reluctant to give up his good seat. He nodded occasionally, knowing that if Hawke did show, she would add to his cover. Hawke would not be expecting him, but having a woman with him added credibility to his clean-shaven, well-dressed appearance. He was a far cry from the "El Diablo" Hawke left for dead in the drug sting setup.

Hunter reflected back to the only time that he'd met Hawke, at an arms bazaar in Paraguay. *He knew I worked as a bounty hunter, but didn't care. Having me around helped his business—he had to keep selling upgrades to his security systems whenever I found ways around his old ones. So, why did he set me up? What turned the tide for him?*

Hunter knew he would have to capture him alive in order to clear his name. But it was just as important to find out why he had tried to kill him. His gut instinct told him that whatever Hawke was working on, it was big.

Just when he was about to give up on his stakeout, the door swung open and in walked Hawke. Hunter turned to his new-found companion and picked up his mundane conversation with her, while he keenly observed Hawke out of the corner of his eye.

Hawke gave only a cursory glance around the room before approaching the main bar, which surprised Hunter. Hawke was either extremely confident of his surroundings or he was distracted. He accepted an Absolut on the rocks from the bartender and turned to face the crowded floor immediately in front of him.

Hunter shifted his position so that his female companion would shield him from direct view. Despite Hawke's laxity, Hunter didn't want to take any chances. He watched as the soldier of fortune downed his drink in two gulps and ordered another one. Hunter quietly decided he would follow him, rather than attempt to take him right away.

A few minutes later, Hawke downed his second drink and headed towards the door, curiously making no attempt to pick up a woman for the night. Hunter was glad, though, that force of habit had brought Hawke to this meat market. As smoothly as possible, Hunter ended his conversation with his bar mate and followed Hawke out of the bar, making sure to remain out of sight.

Hawke walked down the street nonchalantly, without check-ing to see if he had been followed. Hunter, remaining back a fair distance, cagily watched as Hawke approached and unlocked a jet black Explorer. Remaining in the shadows of a storefront, Hunter retrieved a night scope from his jacket pocket. Peering through it, the greenish image revealed Hawke holding the handset of a com-munications device. Hunter recognized it as some type of satellite phone, but was too far away to make out the codes Hawke punched in. He watched as Hawke listened for a moment, then punched in some additional codes. Content that the message had been sent, Hawke replaced the handset and started the engine. Hunter hurried to his vehicle and followed Hawke into Boca's humid night air.

22

△△△

CAROL WALKED INTO Thorn's office, just as he had finished reviewing the status of each company on his list of sales prospects. "Busy?" she asked.

"No. Come in. What's up?" he replied, focusing on getting each company profile back into its proper folder, as Carol sat down across from him.

"I've been thinking about Welborne reneging on his offer of the line of credit."

Thorn nodded and looked up, fixing his eyes on hers.

"He's responsible for making good on his offer, Alec. He said it in our board meeting. Without some more money, we'll be out of business. We should *sue him*." Her previously hidden bitterness towards Welborne became clear in the tone of her last two words.

"I've already spoken to John Brewer about that," he said. "Yes, we could sue him. His offer was recorded in the minutes of our board meeting. The fact that he signed the minutes provides us with all the evidence we need to prove we have a legal contract. But—"

"Then what are we *waiting* for?" Carol interrupted, unable to contain her anger. "Let's get on the phone and tell him what Brewer said. We have a valid contract and we'll sue him to enforce it!"

"That's an option I'd like to save as a last resort." Sensing her intense emotion, he tried to maintain his composure.

"But we can't afford to wait, Alec," her voice pleading for his agreement.

"We have enough cash to last another four weeks," he said, hoping to calm her down. "Maybe even five weeks, if we get a few sales or service contract renewals."

"Let's call him and *threaten* to sue." She leaned forward out of her chair, as she tried to emphasize her point.

"You know Welborne," Thorn said, continuing to match her gaze. "As soon as he hears the word lawsuit, he'll circle the wagons and call his high-priced Palm Beach law firm to investigate. They'll charge him a few thousand bucks and advise him that they want to fight it, which will make him even madder."

He watched Carol closely as she sat back again in her chair, still angry but trying to relax. *She's even prettier when she gets emotional,* he thought. He stood up, walked around his desk and stood in front of her. He gazed into her eyes and watched her anger melt away, replaced by curiosity. He began, "Carol, . . . "

She remained silent, open, but clearly wondering what he would say.

Thorn swallowed nervously, before regaining his composure. "Carol, if we file a lawsuit, his attorneys will stretch out the proceedings as long as possible, knowing we're not in a position to wait. By the time the case is heard, we'd be out of business." He'd subtly, perhaps subconsciously, switched his demeanor to frank and dispassionate.

She nodded her head, but felt somewhat annoyed by his dry, objective tone. She swallowed her quiet sense of hurt. "I understand. All right, the lawsuit is the last resort. What do we do in the meantime?"

Relieved he had maintained his professionalism, he explained his strategy. "I want to give him a few more days to cool off. He might call later this week to see if we're hurting and ready to negotiate. It's important that he know the entire company is united in wanting to hold out for a fair deal. Under no circumstance can we act confrontational—we need to stress that we see him as a friend and just want a fair deal. Eventually, I think he'll come around. I can't call him yet, because he hasn't had time to forget what an asshole he was at lunch."

"Is there anything I can do? Should I call him?"

"No. That would show weakness. On the other hand, if he calls you, you could stress the company's solidarity and your hope that he'll be fair and reasonable."

"You think he'll call me?"

"Normally he wouldn't, since he always likes to speak to the top dog. But, he might, since he didn't get very far with me. He might try searching for a weak link in the chain."

"Don't worry. I'll bite his ear off if I have to," she said.

"Good. Keep those canines sharp."

Carol smiled a satisfied grin and left.

23

△ △ △

Before setting out for revenge, first dig two graves.
—Chinese Proverb

ERICA AND RAVEN were sitting at her worktable discussing strategy, when they heard a knock on the door. "Come in," she said.

It was not the loud banging typical of Hawke, so even before he entered, she knew something was wrong. Seeing his distressed face, a picture of bewilderment, she realized he had failed.

"What's happening is just not possible," he whined. "I put the bomb under the driver's seat of his new rental car and wired it *totally* right. It's the exact same procedure I've used dozens of other times." He looked up, pleading for an explanation from her, but there was none forthcoming. "It didn't go off."

He shook his head in disbelief. "I waited at the far end of the garage to watch. He got in the car and tried to start it up, but the car wouldn't start. He tried again. It wouldn't start. On the third time, it started as if nothing was wrong."

Erica scrutinized him closely for any signs of deception, but recognized quickly he was telling the truth. Raven kept his mouth shut, happy to see Hawke lose face with her, but he was puzzled, as well.

"Bombs don't work with this guy," Hawke said. "I can't explain it."

Erica turned to Raven. "What do you think it is?"

Raven recognized that Hawke's failure offered him a chance to reassume control of the Thorn project. "It's some kind of psychic force he has around him. Only someone able to manipulate these energies will be able to get close enough to take him out."

Hawke hated to see Raven's status re-elevated, but he realized his screwup had set the stage, and that there was nothing he could do about it now.

"You think you can fix this problem?" Erica asked Raven.

He nodded his head confidently. "The Raven can handle it."

Hawke wasn't sure he believed his explanation, but had seen Raven's earlier work, and knew it was beyond him to challenge him about it. He stood by humbly, realizing he'd been relegated to backup. For a moment, he wondered if he should have used his gun and popped Thorn. *It would have kept Raven from getting back into the picture.*

"I'll need to do some research," Raven said with a smile, "but, in a very short while, I'll take care of the Thorn in our side."

24

△△△

SEVENTY-FIVE YEAR OLD Sharir Ghauri descended down the steps of the hidden staircase that led to the subterranean chamber beneath his ranch. At the foot of the stairs, he slid his hand along a crevice in the rock wall to engage a control that slowly slid open the thick, granite door. After he stepped through the opening, the door automatically closed. Walking deliberately to the steel vault door at the end of the corridor, he pressed the codes into the security device and placed his withered hand onto the palm reader. Confirming his identity, the door opened.

Lights came on automatically as he walked to the secure computer and telecommunications equipment—the finest western technology money could buy. Ghauri sat down at the keyboard, typed in a password, and checked for any messages. None. He breathed deeply, trying to control the near-boiling anger rising within him. He picked away at his unkempt beard. "Still no word," he muttered under his breath. Knowing he would be out of direct contact while addressing his graduating students at the Madrassah the entire next week, he decided he could wait no longer. Selecting the appropriate security level, he typed his orders.

＊ ＊ ＊ ＊ ＊

Gecko received the encrypted message, classified "Cosmic," on his secure computer. The ultra-secure Cosmic classification identified the transmission as being 29 levels higher than the Pentagon's "Top Secret" classification. As he inserted his compact disc into the drive, Gecko waited as the complex encryption algorithms did their job. The specialized disc contained a one-time PAD that made it mathematically unbreakable by even the most advanced computers on the planet. His handprint provided the biometric to further ensure that only he would receive the message:

Awaiting package. Without it, the candle will not burn as bright. Need coordinates. Keep all others away.
—The Cleric

Gecko pressed the key to delete the message and automatically overwrite his hard drive with random bits of data to ensure no one would ever be able to retrieve it. He opened his safe and retrieved an envelope containing photos. Then he picked up his phone to call White.

* * * * *

White was sitting at a table near the back wall of the same coffee shop they'd met at earlier in the week, when Gecko walked in and joined him. A nod from Gecko indicated it was safe to talk. White placed a folder on the table.

"I just got these," said White. "It's a coded transmission that originated in Boca Raton and terminated near the Afghanistan-Pakistan border. The approximate coordinates are in the folder, an area of fifty square kilometers. Now that I know what to look for, I can narrow it down further on the next transmission."

Gecko's small, black eyes bore into White, seeking any indication that he was holding anything back.

"What else?"

"Nothing, sir."

"Who knows?"

"No one."

"Has it been logged?"

"Not yet."

"Keep it that way. And delete any references to it, as well. This never happened. Do you understand?"

"Yes, sir, but—"

"No buts!" Gecko said, cutting him off. He rose, taking the folder. "I want to be the first person to know if anything happens in that area." He attempted a smile and started away from the table. "If you keep up the good work, there might be a promotion in it for you."

"Thank you, Sir. As I promised, I'm keeping you informed," White said, "But I can't withhold information."

Gecko stared at White with dark, expressionless eyes. White's discomfort made him speak, "From here on out, I'll have to notify my superiors and follow standard procedures."

Gecko continued to stare at White. He reached into his jacket pocket and took out the envelope containing the photos he had taken from his office safe. He dropped it on the table directly in front of White. "You should have been more discreet."

White looked at Gecko and then at the envelope. Slowly, he took out the photos and thumbed through them. His face betrayed his emotions, moving from curiosity to panic to anguish. He tried stifling his sobs, but could not contain himself.

Gecko said, "Having a male lover . . . is not good for your career." He paused for effect. "Besides, I would hate for anything to happen to Carson."

White peered again into Gecko's eyes. The younger man's distress disappeared, now replaced by hatred.

"I think we're clear on this," said Gecko, before turning and leaving the coffee house.

25

△△△

Dreams are today's answers to tomorrow's questions.
—Edgar Cayce

SOPHIE WAS BUSY arranging flowers when Thorn walked into the shop. "I know I'm early. If you're busy, I'll wait."

"No. I'm done," she replied, putting the finishing touches on her creation. Motioning for him to follow her into the back of the shop, she washed her hands and sat down with him at a brown, formica-topped table containing some paperwork. "What's been happening?" she asked, looking directly into his eyes.

"Last night, I had a dream, but it wasn't like a regular dream. In the middle of it, I knew I was dreaming, but the dream continued. I couldn't tell if I was imagining it, but it seemed real. It was like watching a movie."

"What happened was real. You had a vision," she said.

"A vision? Prophets have visions. I'm no prophet."

Ignoring his remark, she bid him to go on, "Tell me what happened."

"I saw a man in a car following me."

"What kind of car?"

"Big, like a van, but not full size. Black. It was an SUV, like a Blazer or an Explorer."

"Go on."

"He was pudgy, with pale skin—no pigment at all. Like an albino, but he had black hair."

"What about his eyes?"

"Black. There was a bad look about him."

"Who was he?"

"I don't know," he said. "I didn't ask him his name. He was following me."

"Relax," she said. "Close your eyes. Take a few deep breaths."

Thorn did as he was told.

"I want you to concentrate on my voice and continue to breathe deeply. I'm going to count backwards from five to one. You are going to get more and more relaxed. When I get to one, you'll be completely relaxed."

"Five." Thorn continued to breathe deeply.

"Four." He felt himself relax even more.

"Three." He went deeper into a meditative state.

"Two." His breathing grew deep and quiet.

"One. Okay. Now, are you completely relaxed?"

"Yes," whispered Thorn.

"Okay. Let's return to your vision. Are you with me?"

"Yes."

"Who was the man following you?"

"Raven. But it's not just his name."

"Explain."

"It's what he is. He thinks he's a raven."

"Okay. What's he doing?"

"He's just following me. I don't sense I'm in any danger, but he wants something."

"What?"

"I don't know. I don't think he even knows."

"What else can you find out?"

"He has something to do with Kramer."

"Who's Kramer?"

"He was trying to help our company get an important approval. He died in a car accident." Thorn gasped. "He's responsible for his death."

"Relax. Concentrate on your breathing."

Thorn remained agitated.

"Okay, when I count to five you'll be wide awake. One . . . two . . . three . . . four . . . five. You're wide awake."

Thorn opened his eyes with a look of amazement on his face. "I was right there with Kramer! This man made him go to sleep. He tricked him into falling asleep while he was driving."

Sophie nodded. "You've been having that dream a lot. Now you know why."

Thorn looked at her, not understanding how she knew this.

"Your dream was a warning," she said. "He's one of your enemies."

"How? Who is he?"

"Have you ever heard of past lives?"

"I read a book about it. A psychiatrist regressed people back past their childhood into previous lives. Is that what you mean?"

"Yes. You have enemies from past lives and they have been after you for some time."

"Why?" Thorn's body tensed. "If they're willing to kill Kramer, why wouldn't they just kill me?"

"It's not enough for them to just kill you. They want to humiliate you."

"Who are *they*?"

"You tell me. You looked forward. Now look backwards."

"Why don't you just tell me?"

"It's much better if you find out for yourself."

"Can't you give me a hint?"

"You shouldn't rely on me to do your thinking for you. When the time is right, the knowledge you need will come to you."

Thorn looked at her with a slight sense of confusion and helplessness. "How long before I'll understand what's happening, Sophie?"

"Very soon. Your rapid development is being dictated by the circumstances."

"What circumstances?"

"Necessity is the mother of invention," she replied.

Thorn grew frustrated by Sophie's cryptic comments. "Why do you keep dropping hints but refusing to answer my questions?"

"If I were to answer all your questions, you would only have an intellectual grasp of the subject. By making you obtain it spiritually, the knowledge will be much more useful to you. All your answers lie within you." Sophie pushed her chair back from the table and surveyed Thorn. After a moment, she continued. "Trust your instincts. Continue to meditate at least twice a day. You are being sent the information you need. Trust God to provide your answers."

"You act as if you expected this," Thorn said. "You're not worried at all."

"Do you think all I do is arrange flowers?" she asked rhetorically. "Don't worry—you're doing fine."

Thorn left her shop, even more befuddled than before. Walking down the sidewalk toward his car, he reflected on the intuitive precision of Sophie's advice. Thorn shuddered when he realized he'd never told her he meditated.

26

△ △ △

For the love of money is a root of all kinds of evil. Some people, eager for money, have wandered from the faith and pierced themselves with many griefs.
—1 Timothy 6:10

CHAPMAN PICKED up the phone on its second ring.

"Yes."

"It's me."

Chapman recognized Hawke's voice. A brief check confirmed the line was secure. "Go on."

"There's something going on with the computer geek."

"What?"

"He never gets hurt, is what!" he said, with obvious exasperation. "His car caught fire and nothing happened to him. A bomb was planted and it didn't go off. But the fat man's on it. I just thought you should know."

"Anything else?"

"Yeah. My expenses are running higher than I expected."

Knowing Hawke's only expenses were a few phone calls, here and there, Chapman paused before responding. He understood Hawke was shaking him down for more money. "How much more?"

"Another hundred grand should cover them."

Chapman's sneer was not visible to Hawke. He kept his voice flat as he replied, "I'll wire the money today. Same account."

"I'll keep you informed," Hawke said and then hung up.

Chapman remained seated at his desk, closing his eyes and calming himself with a series of deep breaths. He had expected Hawke to hit him up for more money, it being the nature of a mercenary. On the other hand, Chapman would never be motivated by something so distasteful as merely accumulating money. His thoughts trailed off as he picked up the phone to make the arrangements.

Five minutes later, his money wiring concluded, he returned to his recliner and turned his attention to Thorn.

27

△ △ △

Life is a series of awakenings.

—Sivananda

THORN SAT IN A chair in the back of Sophie's shop, intrigued by her explanation for the pulling sensation he occasionally felt in the middle of his forehead. "Your chakras are like miniature satellite dishes, each sensitive to a specific frequency," she explained. "The pulling sensation is caused by my work on your third eye, which I'm doing to remove blocks and increase its sensitivity. This one is used for visions.

"Your seventh chakra, located on the crown of your head, is used to communicate with your higher self and oversoul," she continued. "In spiritually gifted people, the aura is sometimes visible around the head with the naked eye. In that case, it's called a halo."

"What's an 'oversoul?'" Thorn asked.

Sophie paused, as though something far away was calling to her, before replying, "The oversoul is your direct connection to God. It includes your higher dimensional soul-personalities, as well as your past and future lives."

Recognizing that Thorn was still hungry for more of an explanation, she continued, "I'm helping you to reconnect to the higher aspects of yourself. It takes time—it's like sewing with a very fine thread. When I'm done, you'll be able to pull knowledge and information into your conscious mind more easily."

"How will I know whether it's real or if I'm just imagining things?"

"You'll just know." Sophie smiled as she got up. Thorn was not entirely convinced, but he followed her to the door.

Sophie turned as she opened the door to let him out. "Don't worry, just relax. How well you're able to pull in this information will depend, in part, on how well you're able to focus on what's happening *now*."

After leaving her shop, Thorn walked down to the cleaners. He wished he had time to research the scientific basis of her knowledge, figuring it would be easier to accept. On the other hand, it was clear that something was happening—he couldn't ignore the headaches and physical sensations caused by her work.

He glanced out the window of the cleaners and watched her get into her car, marveling at her knowledge and even more so at her lack of pretense. *Was it possible that others were as gifted as she?*

The sound of screeching tires in the parking lot jarred Thorn out of his daydream. He saw the black truck that made the noise veer out into the road, with Raven, the man from his earlier vision, at the helm. Thorn realized immediately that he was following Sophie.

Thorn ran to his rental car, feeling compelled to warn her. He jumped in and tore after them, racing through the first light just after it had turned red. As he sped west on Palmetto Park Road, he was grateful traffic was light that evening, allowing him to gain quickly on them.

Up ahead of him, a set of railroad warning lights began flash-ing. He could see Sophie's car, followed not too far behind by the black truck. As she made it across the tracks, he prayed the ap-proaching train would stop Raven, but he sped up just in time to get underneath the gates. Thorn pulled up to the tracks a few sec-onds later and was forced to sit there helplessly, as the long freight train rumbled by.

He banged the steering wheel with his fist, feeling trapped and as though he'd failed to protect his newfound teacher. *I'm the reason she's in trouble! She was helping me and now she's in danger! Damn!* he thought to himself. He closed his eyes and pictured her face, innocent of the danger. He prayed out loud, "Please, God let me warn her. Please let her be safe."

"*What is it?*"

Thorn opened his eyes to find the source of the voice. It was Sophie, but he couldn't see her.

"*Where are you?*" Thorn thought.

"*I'm in my car. You saw me leave.*"

It was her voice, he was sure of it—but how? "*You can hear me?*" he silently asked.

"*You're coming in clearly.*"

"*This is really happening?*"

"*What do you think?*"

Waves of elation washed over him. "*This is unbelievable.*" In a flash, Thorn remembered why he needed to contact her. "*Raven is after you.*"

"*I know.*"

"*You know?*"

"*Yes. I expected him. I needed to see him in person.*"

"*Are you in danger?*"

"*Don't worry. He won't see me if I don't want him to.*"

The sound of car horns blaring behind Thorn refocused his attention to his immediate environment. The train had passed and he was holding up traffic. Thorn pulled off the road onto a narrow patch of gravel to continue his thoughts with Sophie.

"*Is he still following you?*"

"*No. I just got rid of him.*"

"*Are you sure?*"

"*Yes. I suggested he follow another car that looked like mine. It will be a while before he realizes his mistake.*"

"*Can we communicate like this whenever we want?*"

"*Yes.*"

"*I don't know what to say,*" he thought, recognizing the size of this achievement. Tears streamed down his face, as a feeling of joy overwhelmed him. "*This is the greatest gift anyone has ever given me. Thank you. I don't know what else to say. It's the best day of my life.*"

Thorn could feel her smiling, close to laughing. "*You're welcome.*"

28

△△△

Holding on to anger is like grasping a hot coal with the intent of throwing it at someone else; you are the one who gets burned.

—Buddha

UNABLE TO SLEEP, Erica Buenavista rose from her bed and began pacing back and forth with her hands clasped behind her back. Clad in a blue silk nightgown, she pondered the events of the past few days. *How could Thorn have escaped unscathed, again? Does he have nine lives, like a cat?* she wondered, angered at his tenacity. *If so, I'll just have to use them all up! He's humiliated me once and he will not do so again.*

Tired of pacing, she sat down at her worktable and closed her eyes. Erica's attention drifted toward the source of her rage, as pictures from the past appeared on the screen of her mind.

Standing on the deck of an ancient warship, sailing down the Adriatic Coast, she and her crew were escaping from a ferociously fought naval battle. The scene jumped to a royal palace, where she was dressed splendidly in exotic silk robes. A dark skinned, robed messenger entered, slightly out-of-breath, before he bowed and then handed her a papyrus scroll. Reading the message written upon it, she erupted, raging, "He has defeated Antony, the *true* successor to Caesar, a man *far* more experienced in battle than he!" She paused to read further and then added, "War, I understand. But he *refuses* to meet with me to negotiate. Both Caesar and Antony would have died *a thousand deaths* for a chance to spend a single night with me. Instead, he mocks me, treating me like a

76

commoner." Erica's facial muscles began twitching slightly, as she allowed herself to review this dark and difficult part of her past.

"Well, he will not have *my* head to parade through Rome. Of that I will make sure! And I will return this humiliation some day. Hell hath no fury like a woman scorned. He will see what it is like to reject the Queen of Egypt!"

29

△ △ △

THORN LAY IN HIS bed meditating. Sophie had explained that there was less chance of falling asleep if he remained sitting, but he did not find it difficult to remain awake, even though he lay on his back. He established an especially good connection with Sophie.

"There are times when you don't come in as clearly as you are right now," he thought.

"In what way?"

"It's like you're whispering."

He sensed her smile.

"You know about this?" he probed.

"Yes," she responded.

"It's deliberate?"

"I'm not speaking at all. Do you follow?"

Understanding came to Thorn in an instant. *"This is the difference between spoken and unspoken thought!"*

He sensed her smile. *"It's easier to communicate when two people are both aware of the connection and use spoken thoughts to communicate,"* she thought. *"But this method isn't as flexible. What if I'm busy or too tired to concentrate? Wouldn't it be easier to communicate without relying on the other person?"*

"I see. You were making me stretch." He could sense her smiling again. *"Not bad for a few weeks of training, huh?"*

"Let me ask you, Alec, have you foreseen anyone else coming to help you?"

"What do you mean?"

"*I get the sense that you're going to meet someone who will be a great help to you.*"

"*In what way?*"

"*I can't tell. I'll let you know when I know more.*"

30

△△△

The Lord will protect you from all evil; He will keep your soul.

—Psalm 121:7

AFTER HIS SESSION with Sophie, Thorn got up, left the house, and drove to a nearby French bakery, craving a well-made snack. Moments after he entered, a monster black pickup pulled up outside and a tall man walked in, wearing a Metallica T-shirt with the midriff cropped, displaying a body without a trace of fat. He had long, greasy brown hair and had tattoos of snakes and knives running along his forearms. Tight black jeans, an oversized key chain and heavy boots completed his outfit.

Thorn recognized the headbanger as one of his enemies, though he wasn't sure why. His senses were heightened, but he knew he was not in any immediate danger. The headbanger seemed curious about Thorn, but also wanted to intimidate him. They circled each other in front of the display counter, as they eyed the various pastries, neither man looking directly at the other. A ritual showdown played itself out, with neither man flinching. Each stole glances at the other in the mirror behind the counter. The dark-clad truck driver's piercing blue eyes appeared deep set and sullen to Thorn. Suddenly, he ended their dance by turning around, buying a loaf of bread, and leaving the bakery. Thorn watched him drive off out of sight and then sat down to enjoy his napoleon.

* * * * *

"*Are you out there?*" Thorn thought, after he had made himself comfortable on his recliner.

"*Yes. I'm listening,*" Sophie thought.

"*Are you aware of what happened to me today?*"

"*The man who followed you?*"

"*Yes.*"

"*Tell me what happened.*"

"*A tall, thin man followed me into a bakery. He was not trying to hurt me. It was as if he wanted to see how close he could get to me.*"

"*How close did he get?*"

"*He was standing right next to me. We circled each other, like wild animals, to see who would flinch. I stayed to eat my pastry. He left.*"

"*Who is he?*"

"*I don't know. I thought you might know.*"

"*Concentrate. Picture yourself inside of him.*"

Thorn did as he was told. Slowly he felt as if he were the man following him.

"*What do you feel?*" Sophie asked.

"*Curiosity. He's confused about me.*"

"*Why is he curious?*"

"*He wants to know why I wasn't hurt in my car.*" A shiver ran down Thorn's spine. "*He's the one that set my car on fire!*"

"*Okay. Stay with it,*" Sophie thought.

"*He also put a bomb in my rental car!*" Thorn reflected on his earlier trouble starting the car. "*It wouldn't start at first this morning —that's when it was supposed to explode.*"

"*You see. You are protected from above,*" Sophie thought. "*They can't touch you.*"

Thorn paused a moment to consider this apparent truth.

"*Tell me who he's working with,*" she asked.

"*I'm trying to see if he's friends with Raven.*" Thorn attempted to sense the man's feelings for Raven. "*He knows him. But he hates him. He would kill him if he could, but he's forced to work with him. They hate each other. There is someone else, but I can't see who it is,*" Thorn thought. "*Wait. I can tell it's a woman, but I can't make her out.*"

"*Okay. Tell me what he's trying to accomplish. What's he working on?*"

81

Thorn refocused on the headbanger. *"I'm not getting anything."* He tried again. *"Nothing."*

"Picture him. Tell me what he's doing that's so important."

Images entered his mind. *"Mountains. He's in a desert with mountains all around. Nothing seems to live there. I see caves or maybe they're mine shafts. I can't tell."*

"Where are you?"

"Pakistan." Thorn paused. *"How do I know this?"*

"Don't analyze. Just tell me what you see. What's he doing?"

"He's wearing special clothing. A suit. To protect him against chemicals or something."

"What else?"

"He's in one of the caves. He's working on machinery or some kind of electronic device. It's connected by a long wire to a satellite dish outside. But the dish is surrounded by a haze."

"What is the device?"

"A bomb."

"Be more specific."

"It's a nuclear bomb." Thorn shivered. *"He's working on a nuclear bomb!"*

"Relax," thought Sophie. *"Take a few deep breaths."*

Thorn concentrated on his breathing and broke contact with the images that had come to him.

"Are you all right?"

"Yes." Thorn paused to collect himself.

Sophie remained silent while Thorn regained his balance.

"Did you see what I saw?" he asked.

"Yes. Through your eyes."

"How can he be in Pakistan and in Boca at the same time?"

"He's no longer in Pakistan. This has already happened. What you experienced is called 'remote viewing.'"

"Is it real?"

"Yes. You used your third eye to see with. This is not as uncommon as you would think."

"What do you mean?"

"The military uses this technique to spy on the Russians, among other things."

"How do you know?"

"Never mind. What's important is that you have another tool to accomplish your goals," she thought. "There's one other thing I want you to meditate on."

"Go ahead."

"They're going to get more and more aggressive. You'll need something else to protect you."

"You mean like a gun?"

"No. You don't need that. You stick with spiritual protection," she chided.

"What else should I do, then?"

"I want you to meditate and picture each of your adversaries separately. As you focus on each one I want you to remember whatever word comes to you. That will be your weapon."

"The word?"

"Your voice."

"How does that work?"

"Don't worry about the mechanics. I'll take care of that."

"I just say this word and what happens?"

"You'll see. The louder you say it, the greater the effect will be."

Thorn paused. He had remembered reading about legendary martial artists that were able to throw their opponents without actually touching them. "Is this some kind of martial arts thing?"

"It's the same principle."

"Those guys were all black belts."

"That's not the critical factor. What's important is that they were all able to focus spiritual energy."

Thorn nodded his head and found himself thinking about his recent experience in the light of a famous quotation. *As the pen is mightier than the sword, so is the spirit mightier still.*

31

△ △ △

THORN LAY AWAKE in his bed unable to sleep. Though his body was physically exhausted, the remote viewing experience and communication he shared with Sophie had sent his mind racing. He hoped that by meditating, he could quiet the mental activity and get to sleep.

He breathed deeply and cleansed his energy body using the technique Sophie had taught him. He visualized a white cleansing light flowing from above through his crown chakra and exiting through his feet. He could sense the flow gradually increasing in intensity and velocity until the energetic debris was flushed away. In the midst of his preparation, he felt a slight sensation in his forehead. According to Sophie, this indicated that someone was attempting to contact him. However, the sensation disappeared as soon as Thorn attempted to make contact with the person who'd been reaching out to him.

Irritated, Thorn felt intuitively as though someone were trying to eavesdrop on his thoughts, but feared discovery. Without hesitation, he decided to locate this person.

He returned to his deep breathing, alternately taking in fresh spiritual energy and expelling all negative energy that might have accumulated in his energy body. Now in balance, and with his mind stilled, he kept his mental screen blank, hoping the person would contact him again.

Within a few minutes, he felt the sensation again. Thorn focused on identifying the mysterious inquisitor. Slowly a scene entered his mind: a darkened library or study, with overstuffed chairs whose burgundy leather covers were held together with copper rivets. The room was in a city in the Northeast—Boston, or perhaps New York. In the corner of the room, reclining on an easy chair was an elderly man with shocking white hair, deep in thought. Thorn's visual perspective of the man originated from near the ceiling in the corner of the room.

Thorn knew he was the man trying to contact him. He grew angry and shouted silently, *"Who are you? Who are you?"*

Thorn could see the man's eyes open, indicating he was alarmed. Carefully the man scanned his study. As he looked towards the ceiling, he seemed to lock eyes with Thorn. Suddenly, the man grew frantic. Thorn knew the man had discovered him.

"Who are you?" Thorn thought. *"Why are you spying on me?"*

The man looked about his study, but knew that he could not avoid Thorn. He thought, *"I meant no harm. I apologize. Please forgive me."*

"Who are you?"

"I'm just a businessman," he replied defensively.

"What's your name?"

"Rune Chapman." Thorn tried to place the name, but decided that he had never heard of it.

"Why are you watching me?"

"Please, don't be angry. I was just trying to warn you."

"Warn me? About what?"

"There are some people who are trying to hurt you. I don't know why. I wanted to warn you."

"Why did you retreat each time you sensed me coming?" suspicious of the man's explanation.

"I could tell that you were safe. There was no reason to alarm you by contacting you."

Thorn was skeptical, but he assumed the man told the truth. He wondered, *Is it possible to lie while communicating in this manner? "Tell me about these people."*

"They're mercenaries. For some reason, they're after you."

"What's your interest?"

"Foreign crises upset the capital markets, which is bad for my business. By placing suggestions in their minds, I'm trying to get them to follow a more Godly course of action."

Thorn could sense the man's body relaxing.

"*Could I ask you not to show up unannounced like you did tonight?*" Chapman asked.

"*What do you mean?*"

"*I'm not used to having ghosts appear in my study.*"

"*You can see me?*"

"*You are hazy, but I can see you.*"

"*With your physical eyes?*"

"*Yes, and if my wife were here, you might have given her a heart attack.*"

Thorn paused to consider what he was saying.

"*I might also add, if you're going to visit anyone else, you might want to put some clothes on.*"

Thorn jumped. He became aware that he was back in his bed—naked.

Within seconds, he felt his forehead tingle. He recognized the sensation as coming from Sophie.

"*Are you okay?*" she asked.

"*Yes, I'm fine,*" he thought. "*You saw what happened?*"

She was laughing. "*Yes.*"

"*I was really there in his study?*"

"*Yes.*"

"*How did I do it?*"

"*You left your body.*"

"*That's all there is to it?*"

"*That's it. With more practice, you can make yourself more or less solid.*"

"*He said I was naked.*"

"*You can manufacture clothes by using intention.*"

"*This is wild.*"

She smiled. "*It's not easy to keep track of you anymore.*"

"*I just wanted to see who was contacting me. Do you know this man?*"

"*Yes,*" she answered, then quickly added, "*I have to go.*"

Thorn smiled. *Sophie knew Chapman—he must be the ally she had predicted would appear.*

32

△ △ △

I do not separate people, as do the narrow-minded, into Greeks and barbarians. I am not interested in the origin or race of citizens. I only distinguish them on the basis of their virtue. For me each good foreigner is a Greek and each bad Greek is worse than a barbarian.

—Alexander the Great

THORN ANSWERED THE office phone hoping an investor was calling him back. "Alec Thorn. May I help you?"

"Hello, Alec. It's Martin. I'm glad to see the phones are still working."

"Why wouldn't they be working?" Thorn replied dryly, aware of Welborne's attempt at humor. "It takes at least a month before they turn off the phone for not paying the bill."

The pause at the other end of the line told Thorn that Welborne couldn't tell if he was kidding. "Well, Alec, have you given any more thought to my offer?"

"What offer?"

"The one we discussed at my club."

"That wasn't an offer. That was a request for me to pack up the company and give it to you."

Another silence. Thorn could tell that while Welborne was well suited to bullying cash-starved entrepreneurs, he was not used to dealing with people who stood on principle. "I'll tell you what I am doing to get some money in here, Martin. I'm offering discounts on our service contracts for up front payment; negotiating to license our software to firms that don't compete directly with us; trying to sell new systems; and beating the bushes searching for new investors."

"I don't want to see you mortgaging the company's future by—"

"And I don't want to give the company away to you for next to nothing!" snapped Thorn, cutting him short.

"You'll *still* be out of money by the time one of these hits," he responded in a pompous tone.

"Oh. I forgot to mention. The employees have agreed to defer their salaries in return for stock options."

"That's not your decision to make. It's a board decision," said Welborne.

"It was a board decision to set up the stock option plan. It's my discretion as to how to allocate it."

"We have guidelines, dammit!" Welborne yelled. "You can't just hand out these options willy-nilly! Options are for investors. Anything outside of these guidelines is only for exceptional employees."

"Well, I decided that every employee that agreed to defer his or her salary was exceptional."

Thorn heard the phone slam in his ear. He hoped it wouldn't take another week before Welborne would call back.

33

△△△

Be it known that we, the greatest, are misthought.
—Cleopatra

ERICA ENTERED HER workroom, where Raven and Hawke were waiting for her. She joined them at her worktable. "I don't see any progress being made with Thorn. Why is he still around?"

"It's not my responsibility. You gave the job to him." Hawke pointed to Raven.

"Only after you screwed it up," she said. "And not just once. Twice you couldn't handle him."

She turned to Raven. "What have you learned since *your* screwup? Have you at least been able to find out where his spiritual advisor lives?"

Erica watched Raven wince involuntarily. She knew he needed her praise more than food, so she rationed it out carefully, keeping him on edge, always hungry for approval.

"She hasn't come back to her florist shop in two days. I'm still trying to figure out what we're dealing with."

"What he means is that he's a chicken shit who's afraid of Thorn," Hawke interjected.

"Shut up!" yelled Erica. "You never got close to him, so you're no one to criticize."

"I got near him today."

Focusing her full attention on Hawke, Erica asked, "What do you mean?"

"I followed him into a bakery on Palmetto Park Road. I was standing right next to him."

Both Erica and Raven scrutinized Hawke for signs of deception. "You were standing right next to him?"

"Yeah. I could have reached out and broken his neck in a second."

"Why didn't you *do* anything?" Erica asked.

"There were people around. Besides, you wanted him to handle it," he answered as he pointed at Raven. "I just wanted to see for myself that I could get close to him. There's no reason that he can't be killed just like anyone else."

Erica paused to reflect on Hawke's observation before turning her attention back to Raven.

"That's what I was leaning towards," Raven said. "I don't expect any difficulties. I'll take care of the problem tomorrow."

"Then let's make sure that this is the last page in the Thorn book." She switched her gaze momentarily back over to Hawke. "You set up the cleansing operation." She turned back to Raven and said, "*You*, will handle the actual deed. We'll move to the observation post across from his apartment tonight and hit him tomorrow."

34

△△△

Lo, though I walk through the valley of the shadow of death, I will fear no evil, for thou art with me; thy rod and thy staff, they comfort me.
—Psalm 23

WITH NO NEED TO visit the office, Thorn had allowed himself to sleep late, waking slowly, just after 9 AM that Saturday morning. In between sleep and wakefulness, he drifted along in a tender state of consciousness, in which, as if by magic, everything became clear to him. He saw, with his mind's continually developing eye, that his three enemies were in the next building watching him, and he sensed, quite clearly, that the first battle was about to begin.

Thorn got out of bed and pulled on a pair of gym shorts. Retrieving the *Miami Herald* from outside his apartment door, he went into the kitchen, poured himself some grapefruit juice, sat down at the dining table and began reading the paper. His kitchen, living room and the door leading to the outside hallway were all visible from the building across the way. Realizing that they were monitoring him, he tried to act as normal and unconcerned as possible, despite the tension he felt and his newfound knowledge that "today is the day."

When he'd finished with the newspaper, he retreated to his bedroom, where he was hidden from their view. He showered and shaved while trying to relax, as he prepared for battle. He selected a pair of khaki walking shorts, a white polo shirt and Sperry Topsider boat shoes to wear in the summer heat.

A slight hunger pang reminded him of his need to eat. He laughed inwardly, acknowledging to himself, *Everyone knows that no army fights well on an empty stomach.* He reentered his living area and considered exiting, and then reentering his apartment, just to get them moving. Irritating them would give him some pleasure, but might tip them off. Besides, they didn't know when or if he might decide to leave, so they were forced to wait. He made a silent note of this—*let them wait.*

In his refrigerator, he found some leftover Mu Shu Chicken, which he heated and then ate. Finished with his brunch, he realized again that they would be on the alert for him to leave. He retreated back into his bedroom—*let them wait.*

Though not betraying himself outwardly, he felt the strain. Out of their view, he lay down on his bed to gather his strength. Too hyper to remain still, he rose and went to his bookshelf to find a book that might prepare him for his ordeal. If he'd had a Bible, he might have read it, but the last time he had looked at one was 20 years earlier. He settled on *The Art of War* by Sun Tzu. His classmate had given it to him, but Thorn had never bothered to read it.

He lay down on his bed and paged through the book. Various tactics of war were described—most so obvious they were not useful. In fact, most were so elementary that he had trouble concentrating and he grew sleepy. Closing his eyes momentarily, silent visions quickly filled his consciousness.

Thousands of men were marching at a steady pace across a thin strip of land lying between a long stretch of mountains and a vast sea. The men were part of an army. Thorn could recognize the various parts—the cavalry, the archers, the spear-carriers and the infantry. Almost all had swords. A scout on horseback galloped in from over a distant hill and conferred with the leader, also on horseback.

Thorn could not understand the words, but the meaning was clear. The enemy was swiftly approaching from the rear. His face full of fear, the scout told the leader he estimated that they were outnumbered by at least six to one.

Raising his hand high in the air, the leader halted the procession and turned to face his men. Again, his words were incomprehensible to Thorn, but his message was evident. The moment they had been seeking for their entire journey, the opportunity to confront their enemy was merely a few hours away. Furthermore, the enemy vastly outnumbered them, which would dramatically add to the honor of their victory.

Thorn smiled at the cockiness of the leader, who showed complete confidence to his men. He did not lie or try to minimize their numerical disadvantage. He told them the truth and rallied them, saying they would win great honor with their victory. It was from a place beyond confidence or conviction that he spoke—it was with complete certainty. Waving his hand in another gesture, the men immediately turned around and began heading at double speed towards the enemy. Their goal was to reach a specific place before the enemy did, an area where the mountains nearly met the shoreline.

Thorn felt drawn to the young leader. As the vision continued unfolding, he came to understand the site for the battle was chosen to minimize the enemy's superior numbers by preventing them from circling behind his forces and reducing the number able to come through the pass. The leader's careful site selection would level the playing field.

The army reached their destination and halted. Again the leader took his place at the front, organizing the troops. The bulk of the cavalry were placed on the right, additional cavalry on the left and the spear-wielding phalanx in the middle. His best general was given the job of protecting their left flank by ensuring that no opposing horsemen got around his defense along the shoreline.

Thorn scrutinized the face of the esteemed general. He sat on his horse, emotionless, focused on his task. Though the features were indistinct, he had the feeling that he knew this man. Thorn scrutinized the man's eyes—the windows to his soul. A wave of knowingness came over him—it was the headbanger that had visited him in the bakery the day before.

Thorn returned to his dream. His practice had enabled him to stop and start dreams as though he were replaying a video, but with the added benefit of being able to move around in them and get different views.

His recognition of the general prompted Thorn to examine the leader more carefully. The majority of his views, so far, had been of the leader's back. He attempted to reorient his perspective to see this intense young leader's face. Normally, his intention would be enough to reorient the scene, but in this case, it seemed as if the natural view was from behind. Thorn mentally forced the view to change and was rewarded with a view that showed the young man's features in superb detail.

Thorn studied him. He was young and broad faced, with a reddish tinge to his hair. Again, he peered into his eyes and gasped, as the knowingness came over him. *It's me!* Thorn was jerked back to the present moment.

Thorn rose from his bed shaken. He was familiar with the concept of past lives and had held it as a viable theory. It was no longer a theory. Now, he knew the truth.

He sat down again to consider the ramifications. Had he imagined this vision? Was the stress getting to him? He forced himself to be objective. No. He was sure—he just *knew*, and yet it was not something he would be able to explain to anyone. The sense of knowingness. It was beyond a feeling. It was beyond intuition. It just was.

Thorn returned his attention to his physical body. He had eaten, was well rested and now resumed focus on his task at hand. At 11:45 AM, he decided to contact Sophie to tell her it was time for his first face-to-face encounter with his attackers.

Before he even tried to contact her, he heard her thoughts, *"Don't worry."*

He selected a Florida Marlins baseball cap to shade his face from the noonday sun and grabbed his Oakley sunshades to cover his eyes. The wrap-around style had the added benefit of allowing him to watch for the enemy out of the corner of his eyes without turning his head. It would be harder for them to see whether he was on his guard or not.

Thorn left his bedroom, slowly crossed his living area in full view of the opposing building, opened his apartment door and exited. He did not want them to see him leave too quickly, giving them the impression that he was sneaking out, or that he was even the slightest bit hesitant.

As he walked out the front door of his building, he put on the Oakleys and felt the sun bathe his body with warmth. He crossed the street and walked south along the sidewalk leading to the pier.

On his immediate left was a rock wall that separated the sidewalk from the beach. Palm trees provided shade to the beachgoers who were setting up for their afternoon barbecues. The dense, leafy foliage of the sea grapes shaded the walkway.

Thorn glanced around casually, as if he were simply taking in the scenes. He passed young couples strolling in the sun and rollerbladers skating smoothly along. There was no sign of his enemies, but he knew they were simply waiting for an opportune moment to attack.

Thorn stopped several hundred yards from the pier when he saw a place along the wall where the sea grapes had grown into a dense barrier. He sat on the wall facing the street. To his back, the sea grapes prevented anyone from sneaking up behind him. From this vantage point, he could watch up and down the street for the enemy. Across the street from him was a lightly traveled cross street with many vacant parking spots. Thorn decided that this would be the battle site.

Taking a deep breath and slowly exhaling, Thorn forced himself to relax. Sitting in the shade, dressed in shorts and with a slight ocean breeze, he figured he could just sit there and wait . . . for hours, if necessary.

He exuded the confidence of someone who knew what he was doing—for now he knew he had fought many such battles before. This one only differed in that his sole weapon would be his mind, fueled by a spiritual force he felt certain would lead him to victory.

Thorn watched as a red Camaro pulled up to a parking spot on the cross street. Exiting the car, wearing steel-rimmed Raybans, navy swim trunks, a white crew neck shirt and sandals, was the headbanger. With the grease washed out of his hair and wearing his new outfit, his appearance had been dramatically changed, but Thorn recognized him easily. The man opened the trunk of his car and took out a beach chair and a small, black nylon bag. Thorn wondered how many weapons might be in that bag, but felt no fear or alarm. He knew that this headbanger was only there for backup and to prevent any help from arriving.

A plump girl rode an old 10-speed bicycle slowly past Thorn for the second time. Thorn focused on her and recognized that she was a lookout. Thorn maintained his relaxed posture, while his mind remained focused and razor sharp. He glanced at his watch and saw that fifteen minutes had passed, though it felt like an hour. Everything had slowed down. He remained coiled like a cat waiting to strike out, though it would be his psychic energy, not his physical strength, he would wield.

A cloud passed overhead, casting the entire scene into relative darkness. He asked himself, *Should he take off his shades? No*, came the answer from within, *just wait.*

A small measure of doubt crept into his mind. He wanted everything to take place in the sunlight, where he felt confident. He imagined that darkness and shadows were where *they* worked best. He was not sure—is it fear that I'm feeling?

Thoughts flowed through his mind like a torrent—visions of guns, knives and automatic weapons. "Fear is the mind killer," he remembered, a quote from the book, *Dune. I must dispel the doubt.* He took a deep breath and silently prayed, *"Though I walk through the valley of the shadow of death, I fear no evil, for Thou art with me."*

Thorn felt comforted by his thought and immediately grew more relaxed; still, he remained alert.

A voice came to him. *"Don't worry."*

The voice was not Sophie's. It was a male voice, authoritative, yet amused. Thorn tried to lock onto the source of the communication, but could only sense someone smiling, happy and somehow proud of him.

"Don't worry," he repeated, almost laughing.

Thorn straightened his back, as all doubt left him. He felt at peace. And then he felt a surge of power, as a spiritual force flowed through his body. Slowly, he stretched his body, like a cat lounging in the shade of a tree. He felt even more ready than before. *Let the world know there is a God.*

Thorn turned his eyes slowly to the south and saw Raven, who seemed to be waiting for an elderly couple to pass to keep them from interfering with his mission, but Thorn knew differently. Raven radiated fear. His well-practiced, ambling gait and slow, deliberate body movements could not hide it. Thorn turned his head away from Raven toward the north, wanting him to realize that he was not concerned in the slightest. Thorn knew that Raven would have to confront him. He could sense his thoughts—the headbanger and the woman would consider it cowardly to sneak up on Thorn. He had to prove his valor.

Slowly Thorn turned his head back to the south, taking in the sights. Raven had begun his approach and was only 20 feet away. Thorn turned his head to gaze across the street. Letting his eyes move from side to side, he could see that no one else was in view. Without turning his head, he focused on Raven, who slowed. Thorn watched vigilantly, expecting him to reach under his baggy shirt and grab a gun or a knife. Raven stopped in front of Thorn, but hesitated to look at him. Thorn took off his sunshades and stared at Raven with his naked eyes, ready to pounce. Raven started to turn towards Thorn, then stopped. He opened his mouth, but no words came out. He again tried to face Thorn, but could not. Unable to speak or even look at Thorn, he slowly moved on. He stopped and sat down on the rock wall 50 feet from Thorn.

Thorn broadcast the message to Sophie. *"He chickened out and ran away! He couldn't even look at me!"*

His initial reaction was to pursue the retreating Raven and attack. He stopped himself with the discipline of his mind and thought through his alternatives. *Should I follow Raven and destroy him, removing him from future battle? Or should I leave him disgraced in front of his army and let them wonder why Raven had backed off and what would have happened had Raven chosen to engage me?* In a flash, he knew his best decision would be to do nothing. Just like an exterminator, he would let the cockroach return to the nest with the poison of cowardice to infect the others.

Thorn waited unmoving. He wanted there to be no mistake that Raven had retreated. He would give him a chance to re-engage, but Thorn knew that the battle was over. Within minutes Raven left, using a hand motion to signal his mission was aborted.

Thorn waited until Raven was out of sight before getting up from the wall and departing. Adrenaline was still flowing through his body.

The voice returned. *"I told you not to worry,"* he said laughing.

* * * * *

Thorn returned to his apartment. The adrenaline had stopped flowing and he grew tired. He retreated into his bedroom, laid himself down on his bed, and began reflecting on his victory.

He closed his eyes and pictured the current scene of the enemy camp, which came to him clearly. The woman, the apparent leader, was frowning, unnerved. Raven was attempting to rationalize his retreat. The headbanger's emotions were uncontrollable. The conversation came to Thorn in his mind.

"You ball-less sack of shit!" the headbanger yelled. "You chickened out. We had 12 men cleanse the area and you just chickened out." He punctuated his comments by taking two handguns and a switchblade out of his nylon beach bag and slamming them on the table.

"I didn't chicken out," said Raven. "Something was wrong. It was a trap."

"Bullshit!" yelled the headbanger. "We had enough men with enough fire power to take on an entire marine regiment and you were too scared of one goddamn, unarmed geek to take him out." He shook with rage at the cowardly excuse of a soldier who shared the same room as him.

The woman spoke for the first time. Thorn could sense that she agreed with the headbanger, but was trying to arrange a truce. "All right, already. This is not a big deal. It didn't work out. We'll just pick another time."

"No way," said the headbanger. "I'm not going to waste my time and my men's time ever again on that ball-less creature. You don't often get opportunities like this. All he had to do was walk up to him, put the gun to his head and pop," he said, using his hand as a prop.

"How about I just pop you," Raven said in a burst of bravado, as he pulled his Glock out from under his shirt and approached the headbanger.

The headbanger glanced at Raven and spoke with disgust. "Put that away before I shove it up your ass."

"Are you afraid I'll use it?" asked Raven, as he walked closer.

The headbanger turned away and, in a reflex, spun around and lashed out with his right hand, knocking the gun out of Raven's hand. With his left hand, he grabbed Raven by the throat and threw him against the wall. With Raven dazed, he picked up his own Glock from the table, grabbed Raven by the hair and forced his gun into Raven's mouth.

"You want to open your mouth again?" He mocked the chubby man whose eyes were bulging out of their sockets in fear.

"Enough!" yelled the woman. She knew better than to get in the middle of the fight, but her yelling was enough to get the head-banger's attention. He let go of Raven, gathered his weapons and left the room.

Raven tried to explain himself. Thorn could not understand the words. The fear felt by Raven and the lack of conviction in his words made understanding difficult.

His blather annoyed the woman. She glared at Raven with a message that made it clear she did not believe him and that he should be thankful he hadn't been killed on the spot by the headbanger.

Raven tried to talk himself into believing that there were ambushers hiding behind Thorn and that he was wise to call off the attack.

Thorn got angry as he followed the conversation. *He's lying*, he thought, careful not to project his thoughts. He got up and walked to his apartment door, confident that the enemy scouts would report his exit. He would make it crystal clear that someone was a coward.

Thorn exited his building and crossed the street to a wooden deck that allowed beachgoers to cross to the beach without disturbing the newly planted sea oats. In the middle of the bridge, in full view of his enemies, he stopped and sat on the rail. He was not wearing a hat, nor any sunshades. He surveyed the surrounding territory, as would a king. His body language made it clear that this was his realm.

Thorn tuned into the thoughts in the room across from his apartment. The scouts pointed out Thorn's location. Everyone in the room kept silent, taking turns watching Thorn with binoculars through the tinted windows of their camp.

The headbanger had reentered the outer room when he was told of Thorn's movement. "What's he doing?" he asked, not expecting any reply.

In Thorn's mind, he could see the woman's face reveal her confusion. She was at a complete loss for words. She took the binoculars again and watched.

The headbanger continued to repeat his question, "What's he doing?" while shaking his head.

Raven said, "It's another trap. See, I told you. I was right."

The headbanger glanced at Raven with disgust before retreating from the window. Thorn did not attempt to send any thoughts that would confirm that he was aware of their conversation.

While the woman scanned him with the binoculars, Thorn could sense an inward smile in her mind. She understood Thorn's purpose, but she could not tell if it was conscious or instinctive. He was a warrior, that much she was sure of.

Raven continued his attempts at rationalization. "The good news is that I foiled their ambush. The bad news is—"

"Shut up!" the woman yelled, turning to glare at him. "The bad news is that he has more courage in his little finger than you have in your entire being!" She retired to an interior room.

Realizing that they were not going to act, Thorn left his perch and returned to his apartment.

35

△ △ △

To the rulers of the state then, if to any, it belongs of right to use falsehood, to deceive either enemies or their own citizens, for the good of the state: and no one else may meddle with this privilege.

—Plato

IT WAS SUNDAY MORNING and Thorn had just returned from his routine swim in the ocean across the street from his apartment. After showering, he laid down on the couch to relax. As he stared up at the ceiling fan, slowly spinning above him, a tingle in the middle of his forehead alerted him that someone was trying to communicate with him. After a few deep breaths, he realized Chapman was contacting him.

"Mr. Chapman? Why are you contacting me? I hope it's not to warn me about more danger."

"No, but I saw what you did yesterday."

"You were tuned in?"

"Yes. That was very brave."

"Thanks," Thorn thought.

"What sort of business are you in?" Chapman asked, changing the subject.

"We offer wireless Internet access."

"How's business?"

"At the moment, not so hot. We were inches away from a $10 million contract that would have been a tremendous boost to our company's sales and profitability. Unfortunately, the deal fell through at the last minute, when our contact at the FCC died unexpectedly."

101

Thorn wondered if he should explain the cause of Kramer's death, but reasoned that if Chapman knew about his encounter the previous day, he likely knew about the death.

"Do you need any money?"

"Yes. We're actively seeking financing."

"You mean you're broke and are desperate," Chapman teased.

"I wouldn't say we're desperate, but we need cash."

"How much are you looking for?"

"There are two corporations talking about a $2 million stock deal with us. We just need some bridge financing until I can close one of these deals."

"How far would another $50,000 take you?"

"That would give us a month of breathing room and enable us to secure financing on advantageous terms." Thorn paused before asking, *"You said you were a businessman. Are you an investor?"* Thorn asked. Though the means of communication was new, Thorn did not want to miss out on a chance to pitch a prospective investor.

"Yes. I manage quite a few funds."

"What's the name of your firm?"

"You wouldn't recognize it if I told you. My clients prefer to avoid publicity."

"Can I send you our latest business plan?"

"That won't be necessary. You live in Boca Raton?"

"Yes. North Ocean Boulevard."

"You're in the phone book?"

"Yes."

"I'm going to send you a check for $50,000 to ease the pressure."

Thorn's reaction was part shock, part joy. *"Don't you need me to sign something?"*

"No. I saw what you can do and want to help. I'll contact you after you have stabilized your situation. God Bless."

36

△ △ △

Not even a mighty warrior can break a frail arrow when it is multiplied and supported by its fellows. As long as your brothers support one another and render assistance to one another, your enemies can never gain the victory over you. But if you fall away from each other, your enemy can break you like frail arrows, one at a time.

—Genghis Khan

SOPHIE WAS SITTING IN church, waiting for the service to begin, when a short, well-built man caught her eye as he came up the aisle. She watched his striking blue eyes with interest, noticing that his energy field was particularly strong. As he approached and sat down across the aisle from her, he held her glance longer than would normally have been polite. She knew that he wanted to communicate with her.

Sensing no danger, she focused on the man to determine his intentions. She was surprised to find that he actually *expected* her to probe him.

"*Who are you?*" she thought.

"*Hunter. My friends call me Bobby. That's what you can call me.*"

"*You were looking for me. Why?*"

"*The person I'd like to speak to is under close surveillance. I'm trying to find out why.*"

"*Who is this person?*"

"*Alec Thorn.*"

"Should I know him?"

"It's okay. I'm on your side. The terrorists who are after him left me for dead. I want to stop what they're doing, and my desire to repay them has led me to seek out this guy, Thorn. They're after him and it may help me to know why."

She sensed he was telling the truth. "Tell me what you know and I'll see if I can help," Sophie thought.

"They're trying to extort money from NATO in exchange for not selling a nuclear device to terrorists. The three principals are all psychopaths. If they're successful, you can forget about any of your so-called freedoms that we take for granted in the United States. The country will be operating under a police state, with constant threats of terrorist attacks used to gain the public's acceptance of these new anti-terrorist laws."

He paused as the congregation rose to sing the opening hymn. After several words of prayer from the priest, the congregation sat down. Hunter thought, "I don't know where the bomb is. All I know is that they're fixated on Thorn. I watched one of them follow him to your shop."

"Go on."

"In addition to leaving me for dead, they also set me up. The CIA has orders to use whatever force is necessary to apprehend me. I can't let them do that until I get those three terrorists and clear my name. Until I do, I have to rely on just a handful of trustworthy men."

The two of them rose to sing another hymn. During the prayers that followed, Sophie silently asked, "How can I help you?"

"Can Thorn communicate like this?"

"Yes."

"Put me in touch with him. I need to hook up with him so that, for a period of time, he'll telegraph his every move to me so that I can pick those guys off, one by one. Yesterday, at the beach, I had no warning and was powerless to do anything. I watched them cleanse the area. They were planning to kill him."

"I know." Sophie smiled as Hunter turned to look at her. She could sense the puzzlement in his eyes. "Don't worry about Alec; he knows what he's doing."

He let her comment go without arguing. Hunter mused, *If he knew what he was doing, then he deliberately walked into their trap.* "*We should work together,*" he telegraphed to Sophie.

"*Yes.*"

"*One last thing,*" thought Hunter. "*Why are they after him?*"

"*It's personal. The woman has a grudge against him.*"

Hunter seemed satisfied. In his line of work, revenge was a powerful motive. At the same time, Thorn did not seem like someone who had ever crossed one of them. If he had dealings with them, he wouldn't be busting his ass starting a new company—not when it's so much more lucrative to sell drugs or weapons.

Sophie interrupted Hunter's musings. "*I'm ready to introduce you to Alec, now.*"

Hunter locked into her thoughts again and could sense Thorn was also connected. "*Alec, this is Bobby Hunter,*" she thought. "*He's here to physically capture your tormentors.*"

Thorn focused his attention on the man Sophie introduced. Intuitively, Thorn could sense a feeling of playfulness coming from the man—not the kind of attitude you'd expect from a bounty hunter. "*You're here to capture them?*" Thorn asked.

"*That's right.*"

"*Where were you, yesterday? Did you take the day off?*"

"*No. I was busy watching you nearly get your ass killed.*"

Thorn laughed. "*Don't wait for me to do your job. Feel free to pick them up whenever you like.*"

"*Unfortunately, I'll need your help,*" Hunter explained. "*From now on, I want you to telegraph your every move to me. They'll be contacting you in the next day or so. Try to set up a meeting at the Aruba Beach Café.*" Hunter sent Thorn an image of the well-known café on Ft. Lauderdale's beach, as well as the verbal thought. "*I'll have a team of men positioned there to protect you and hopefully to capture them.*"

"*Okay. Anything else?*" Thorn asked. "*I have to go.*"

"*No,*" Sophie answered. "*Go ahead.*"

Hunter turned to look at Sophie as the service ended.

"*How will I get in touch with you?*"

"*Just like you're doing now. I'll know it's you. If I need you, I'll ring for you.*"

"*How?*"

His answer came in the form of a splitting pain in his forehead that felt as though a drill was boring into his skull. He smiled, thinking, *She's pretty tough for such a little lady.*

37

△ △ △

IT WAS SOMETIME after 8 PM and Chapman sat back in his recliner meditating. Every Sunday he followed a similar routine. In the morning, he would discharge his religious obligations by attending church, shaking hands with the parishioners and going to dinner with his wife at her mother's house in the late afternoon. In the evening, while his wife watched television, he would retire to his study to relive what once was and to imagine what might have been.

Deep in trance, he could see Anka—tall, blonde and beautiful. If only he had met her a year earlier, prior to her marriage. Having instantly fallen in love with her, he would have married her on the spot.

Sadness filled his heart, knowing he had missed his opportunity to experience true love. When they met, she was already married to an Argentine general. At the time, Chapman was a mere investment advisor. It seemed totally unjust to him. The pen may be mightier than the sword, but not in that country. There, power ruled. He had to obey the barbarian General or lose his job.

It had taken him 35 years, but he had righted the situation. Now the generals and politicians bowed to him. The troubles of states would not end until philosophers would become kings or until kings would become philosophers. He smiled. Even better was when the kings bowed to the supreme philosopher—a humble man like himself. Plato's *Republic* would soon become a reality.

It was too late, though, to save Anka. But at least he could save Erica.

38

△ △ △

GECKO TOOK HIS SEAT at the large oval-shaped table prominently situated in the middle of the conference room at NATO headquarters in Brussels. The US Secretary of Defense had allowed him to attend in his stead. Even better, he had accepted Gecko's advice to delay any decision to take action while NATO forces tried to find the nuclear device.

The Secretary General took his position at the head of the table. "Gentlemen, we have one week to decide whether to pay the $3 billion ransom to Buenavista. If we pay, the nuclear device will be disarmed and handed over to us, with no one the wiser. If we don't, the device will be sold to the highest bidder."

"How do we know they really have a nuclear device?" asked the German Defense Minister.

"The Russians picked up six men on the Russia-Kazakhstan border," responded the Secretary. "All of them were suffering from acute radiation sickness. They determined the nuclear material came from Chelyabinsk, a production facility in the Southern Urals, near the Kazakhstan border."

"Is the plant still operational?" asked the German.

"All five reactors have been shut down," the Secretary replied. "Unfortunately, it's one of two principal storage areas for weapons grade material."

He added, "A man fitting Hawke's description accepted delivery. He left with a Russian military convoy and vanished once he made it over the Kazakhstan border."

"How much material did they get?"

"Five kilograms of weapons grade plutonium."

"Is that enough for a bomb?"

"The bomb dropped on Nagasaki contained 13.6 kilograms and produced a 21 kiloton yield." The Secretary's face registered the gravity of what he was explaining. "Nuclear technology has come a long way since then. The use of tampers, reflectors and boosters can dramatically increase the yield."

"They have this capability, then?" asked the German, anxious for the Secretary General to get to the bottom line.

"Yes," he declared. "There is also the problem of a missing nuclear scientist, one of the designers of the Soviet's ADMs."

"ADMs?"

The Secretary turned to the rest of the group and elaborated. "Atomic Demolition Munitions. As many of you know, the Soviets had a program, similar to one in the US, to produce so-called suit-case nuclear devices. These compact devices weighed less than 35 kilograms. If they have this scientist, they have the means to con-struct a device with a 20 kiloton yield."

"Any idea where the scientist is?" questioned the French Defense Minister.

"He was last seen heading to Thailand," replied the Secretary. "We think he's been kidnapped."

"Thailand? What for?" asked a senior Belgian official, sound-ing perplexed.

"He answered an ad for a mail order bride and left Russia to pick her up. The ad found in his apartment was placed by a com-pany that doesn't exist."

No one dared laugh, but looks of disbelief spread among the delegates' faces. The Secretary General said, "The Russians have pledged their full cooperation. Vympel nuclear counter-terrorist commando units are at our disposal."

"Bloody well, they *should* be. It's their damn fault!" barked the British Defense Secretary, banging his fist on the table. A clamor of concerned voices rose up, as others at the table began chiming in.

"Gentlemen, please," shouted the Secretary General. "We have no time for finger-pointing. Let's get back to the issue at hand."

"Do we have any idea where the device is?" asked the German Defense Minister.

The Secretary paused, looking around the table before responding, "Somewhere in Central Asia."

"Worst case, what happens if it explodes?" asked the British Secretary.

"That depends on the exact location. Thousands would die instantly. The prevailing winds would carry the radiation eastward. In the end, millions would die throughout Central Asia, Kashmir and Western China."

"Not to be insensitive," replied the Englishman, rather coldly, "but so what if some terrorists kill a bunch of Muslims? Our mission isn't to save the Muslims. We could just chalk it up to a Pakistani nuclear test gone bad, or else blame it on India."

Gecko hid the smile that formed at the corner of his mouth. The Secretary General stared at the Englishman with open disgust. "How many Muslims left alive are going to listen to your story that it was an accident? What happens when talk of holy war hits the streets of all our Arab allies? Are you ready for World War III?"

The British Secretary frowned, but said nothing.

"Even worse, what happens if they sell it to some Islamic fundamentalists? They've already contacted Saddam and North Korea."

The French Defense Minister broke the silence, "Gentlemen, I'm afraid we have another problem. As you know, there are enormous oil and gas reserves in the Caspian Sea, which are just coming on line. The Kashagon superfield is the largest oil discovery of the last 20 years. The onshore Tengiz oilfield is nearby. If the blast is anywhere close to these fields, the radiation will render these reserves unusable for fifty years. Without these reserves, our western nations will be out of fuel in 20 years."

The room remained silent before the British Secretary asked, "Why don't we just pick up Buenavista and bring her in for questioning? Our people can be *very* persuasive."

The Secretary General said, "They're employing a 'dead man' device. If they don't signal the device at set intervals, it will detonate."

"Can't we track the signals? Can't the NSA monitor these signals with their satellites?" asked the Belgian official.

All eyes turned to Gecko. "The NSA has moved two satellites into orbit over the area," he answered, shifting himself into a more authoritative body posture. He cleared his throat and raised his voice. "The SIGINT satellites haven't picked up anything yet. They may be using some sort of low-tech signaling system. But we're on it."

As there were no responses coming from the group, Gecko added, "I suggest we take a few days to report back to our governments and await further orders. Our reconnaissance satellites are combing the area scanning for ground anomalies. We have Special Forces and Nuclear Emergency Search Teams assembled in the area, waiting to pounce on any likely site. We're pouring all our resources into this hunt and we expect to succeed."

The Secretary General agreed and adjourned the meeting for 72 hours.

39

△△△

[Upon being offered half of the Persian Empire in ex-change for a treaty] Parmenion spoke up and said: "If I were Alexander, I should accept what was offered and make a treaty." Alexander cut in and said: "So should I, if I were Parmenion."

—Diodorus Siculus
Bibliotheca Historica

HER PHONE CALL came at 9:15 AM. Thorn had been expecting it.

"Mr. Thorn?" asked a sensual feminine voice.

"Yes. Who's calling?" he asked, aware that it was the woman.

"Mr. Thorn, this is Erica Buenavista of Global Investment Funds. I understand you're looking for some capital to expand your business."

"That's right. How did you get my name?" asked Thorn, curious as to the lie she would tell to justify her call.

"Jim Kramer at the FCC had mentioned you had some innovative technology that might be of interest to our investment group. Perhaps we could get together and discuss your plans?"

Since Kramer was dead it would be impossible to check out her story. It didn't matter; he knew she had no intention of investing in his company, and that this was merely a pretext for a meeting. Investors would seldom meet with a company without having first reviewed a complete business plan, and she had not asked for one.

"I'll be tied up this week," Thorn responded, guessing she was not the type to want to wait. "Perhaps you can call next week and we can set something up."

"I was hoping to meet sooner. I'll be leaving town later this week. Could we squeeze in a meeting before then?" she asked, her voice flavored with a subtle plea to say yes.

"How about lunch today?" he asked, catching her off guard. "I need to go to Ft. Lauderdale this afternoon. I could meet you at the Aruba Beach Café at 12:30." Thorn knew that with so little time, Erica would be unable to prepare an elaborate ambush. Hunter's people would have the advantage. "Would that fit your schedule?"

She preferred to have her meetings in the evening, when most people, fatigued from a day of work, would be more susceptible to her will. Her experience also cautioned her that she should be the one to pick the time of the meeting, but she knew that no one would try to capture her as long as she had the nuclear guarantee. At the same time, Thorn was an amateur and it was possible he really had to go to Ft. Lauderdale. "That sounds fine," she replied, "I'll see you there, Mr. Thorn. I'm a blonde and I'll be wearing a red dress."

* * * * *

Thorn arrived at Aruba at 12:30. Though he had never met Erica, he felt sure he would recognize her from the image in his mind, regardless of whether she'd be wearing the red dress she'd mentioned. He paused at the hostess stand to scan the crowd of diners. Several groups of men and women that fit the profile of covert agents were seated throughout the café. The air was tense, but he could not tell whose side they were on, as none presented any immediate danger.

Eventually Thorn's eyes came to rest on an attractive blonde wearing a red dress, sitting with two men at a far table overlooking the beach. She caught his eye and smiled. Thorn moved across the restaurant to her table. He recognized the dark haired one as Raven. The taller, light haired one was the headbanger he'd encountered. Shorn of his greasy locks, he appeared as a respectable businessman.

Thorn nodded to her as he sat down. "I was not expecting additional guests."

Erica sensed that Thorn understood the true motive for the meeting. There was no need to maintain the pretense of a prospective investor meeting or to fake formal introductions. "This is Richard Hawke," she said, gesturing to the tall one, "and this is Karl Waldron," pointing to Raven.

In a polite, conversational tone, Thorn pointed to Raven and said, "I would love to continue our meeting, but not so long as this gutless piece of trash is sitting at the same table as me."

Erica examined Thorn, concealing her surprise. She would have liked to keep Raven around. As a rule, she preferred to have her subordinates handle the preliminary discussions to enable her to sit back and size up her opponent. In this instance, she figured she could do without Raven. She maintained her polite expression while turning to Raven and dismissing him with a nod. Raven's face betrayed the insult and the dishonor he felt, but he left without a word. Hawke tried to maintain a poker face, but Thorn detected the hint of a smile. He knew Hawke would never have invited a coward to a Council of War.

"What is it you want?" Thorn asked.

Erica hid her annoyance at his blunt manner. Everyone knew she was not interested in his company, but there was no need to state the obvious. "I have a proposition for you, which I think you'll like." She studied Thorn, knowing he would not be easily charmed, but she was confident of her persuasive abilities. Remaining cool and calm, she tried to establish a mental link that would lead him into her web.

Thorn sat without speaking or betraying his emotions, feeling no need to fill the gaps of conversation. She had called the meeting. He knew quite a few people were carefully watching this conversation. He was tempted to look around, but focused on Erica.

Realizing that he was not cooperating, Erica said, "I understand you are seeking $2 million in funding for your company. I would guess that this company represents a starting point for your business career. As soon as your company is self sufficient, you will want to parlay your profits and reputation into larger ventures." She paused to let her words sink in.

"Suppose we were to shortcut this process and set you up with a fund that would let you finance fifty companies just like yours without having to wait for the first one to succeed. Would that be of interest to you?"

Thorn could do the math in his head; *she implied funds of $100 million.* He tried not to show his pleasure at the prospect. "I would have complete authority for all investment decisions?"

"Yes."

"Go on."

"I am also guessing that after you make a name for yourself and put some money into your pocket, you might shift your attention to other fields—perhaps politics."

Thorn's interest was piqued. He was repulsed by the favors handed out to special interest groups and had dreamed of changing the system someday, but had put those thoughts out of his head. First, he needed to establish himself in the business world. "What do you have in mind?"

Erica smiled as she watched his resistance melt. "It may take another 10 years, but how would you like to be President?"

Thorn was speechless; it sounded ludicrous. *No one can make you President,* he thought. But the certainty of her voice underscored her belief that it was entirely achievable. "How are you going to do that?"

"You let us worry about that. We are quite adept at manufacturing heroes—people that arise out of nowhere to solve a seemingly unsolvable problem." She smiled. "You see, if you cause the problem, you can solve it—or have your representative solve it, as the case may be."

Thorn paused to let the message sink in. *She has done this before. How many of the crises around the world were provoked or made worse by these people? Do they intend to continue to disrupt and terrorize the world until they're called in to restore order? She mentioned 10 years. Was that the time period in which the instability would be raised until the civilized world cried uncle?*

Thorn returned to his original thoughts. "Assuming you can deliver on your end, what is it you want from me, in return for money and the Presidency?"

"There are many companies we come across that might need some investment capital down the road. We'll pass along these leads to you and hope that you'll pay close attention to these firms' needs when you make your investment decisions. As for the Presidency, we just like to have people we can trust in positions of power, vetoing unwise legislation, etc. We regard it as an insurance policy."

The implications to Thorn were obvious. He would be famous, a multi-millionaire and President of the United States. In return, he would be asked to invest in companies doing business in the gray areas of commerce. Politically, he might be asked to vote for Erica's interests, which might not match those of the nation.

No one was asking him to do anything illegal. He could ensure that he had final authority on any investment decisions. If he entered politics, he could always vote for what he thought was right. The question was, would he be in control?

This seemingly ideal situation had a chink, however. "What's to keep me from changing my mind after I get the money?" he asked.

He cringed inwardly as the question came out of him. *What's to stop them from simply killing me?* He tried not to show that he recognized the stupidity of his question.

Erica was aware of the obvious answer to the question and that Thorn also knew it. She preferred not to address unpleasant thoughts or activities. That was why she had Hawke. But she had led the discussion exactly as she had planned. Thorn knew the obvious answer and his defenses would be lowered for her new approach.

"We anticipated that your goals and perspective might shift down the road, which is why we would insist on a contract, of sorts."

Thorn's face revealed his bemusement. "Are you really giving me complete discretion or am I to be controlled by some side agreement that grants you the right to veto all of my decisions?"

"You will have complete discretion, as I already stated. The type of contract that I am referring to is unrelated to your work."

Thorn leaned back in his chair. Erica recognized his confusion and waited for him to ask for clarification. "You speak of a contract that will ensure I cooperate with you, yet you say this contract does not concern my work." He paused again and focused on her riddle. Finally, he relented and asked, "What is it you have in mind?"

Erica smiled and tried to seduce him with her enchanting eyes, eyes that reduced most men to helpless idiots. "The contract I am referring to is a marriage contract. Through marriage, we will grow together. By exposing you to my contacts, you will come to see that this way is for the best. It is the simplest way to gain cooperation."

Thorn's mouth hung open. *Is she kidding? Perhaps testing me?* He looked at her while trying to remain noncommittal, but his puzzlement showed on his face. She held his look with a half-smile, neither confirming nor denying his thoughts. She was accustomed to dealing with men. "You're serious?"

"Very." Her tight red dress hiked up a few inches on her tanned legs, as she shifted herself around in her chair to more fully face him, a maneuver he couldn't help but enjoy watching.

"I must say I'm surprised." Thorn stalled to gather his thoughts. "I don't know how to respond. I guess I should be flattered, but I just met you. We barely know each other." Thorn hesitated as he spoke, acknowledging that, though it was true that he barely knew her, she obviously knew him.

"Don't worry," Erica said. "We'll get to know each other. And the more you know, the happier you'll be." A raw feminine sensuality oozed from her lips and eyes as she spoke, making it seem to Thorn that she was closing in for the kill. Still, she was also quite mindful about biding her time.

"I'm no expert on marriage," Thorn said, "but aren't you supposed to fall in love before you decide to get married? Am I missing something?"

Erica smiled. She was not used to dealing with such naive opponents. "Do you think today's financial and political dynasties have been perpetuated by haphazardly relying on love? First, you find a suitable mate, then you make the arrangements. Love is something that blossoms in time."

Thorn listened to her deliver her lines carefully. She placed little importance on love, adding references to the subject for the benefit of Thorn's innocence. "Maybe, I'm just old-fashioned."

Thorn wondered to himself, *Who is this person who had spent tens of thousands of dollars attempting to break my spirit? Her marriage proposal is just another attempt to control me. But why?*

Thorn gazed at her with unfocused eyes. In his mind, her image transformed itself. She was now the Queen of Egypt, bedecked in colorful silks and jewels, lounging in her royal palace. In her hands were the puppet strings used by puppeteers. Attached to the strings were Caesar and Antony.

The image disappeared and his normal vision returned. Thorn understood that, as a woman, she could not become the most powerful leader in the modern world. She would have to exert her influence from behind the scenes, or through her husband, as she had done when she charmed Caesar and Antony.

Hawke remained silent during Thorn's visions, unable to tap into his thoughts. "Half a loaf is better than none," he said, attempting to sway Thorn. "I would take that deal, if I were you."

Thorn turned to Hawke. "And so would I, if I were you."

40

△ △ △

WHILE STILL AT THE office at 6 PM, Thorn tried to organize his thoughts for the next day. He took a deep breath and let it out slowly as he tried to calm his nerves and focus on his business. Grabbing a notepad, he began jotting down a list of activities that needed doing.

His phone rang, momentarily interrupting him. He sighed, then answered his phone. "Alec Thorn. May I help you?"

"Alec, this is what I want you to do."

He recognized Sophie's voice. She had never called him before. He knew why—the phones were all bugged. Besides they could communicate with thought.

"Why—"

"Do you remember the oil that I gave you?" she asked, cutting him off.

"Yes."

"Where is it?"

"At home."

"I want you to get it and use it the way I told you. Do you understand?"

"You want me to go home and get it?"

"Yes. Do it now," she said and then promptly hung up.

Walking out of his building, Thorn was greeted by an unusual sight. He wondered if anyone else noticed the large number of water delivery trucks parked outside the building, or that neither of the two cable TV trucks parked across the street were from the company that regularly serviced the neighborhood. *It's as if everyone is walking around in a daze,* he thought to himself.

Thorn got in his car and turned onto A1A to drive the five miles to his apartment. Traffic was light, so he attempted to contact Sophie mentally to ask why she was acting in this unusual manner.

"*Yes. I'm here. Are you on your way?*" she asked.

"*I'm almost at my apartment. Why did you call me on the phone?*"

"*I'll tell you later. Just get the oil and wait in your apartment until I contact you.*"

Thorn parked the car and went upstairs. He found the oil and used it as she had directed—two drops behind each ear. He sat down in his recliner to meditate. Breathing deeply, he re-established contact with Sophie.

"*What's going on?*" he asked.

"*Watch.*"

Thorn tuned into the pictures she was presenting to him in her mind. He saw himself driving to his apartment. The image shifted several car lengths back when he stopped at the traffic light just down the street from his building. The car directly behind him had apparently stalled. The driver of a late model black car attempted to back up and go around this car, but was blocked by a cable TV truck that had pulled up closely behind it. In a matter of seconds, two men with guns drawn approached the three occupants of the black car from both sides and ordered them out and into the truck. A third man got into the black car and all three vehicles drove off. The entire episode was over and done with in less than 45 seconds.

"*We've been able to pick up three more of them. Only three more to go,*" thought Sophie.

"*You used me as bait.*"

"*We had to.*"

"*Why didn't you tell me first?*"

"*There was no time. Just now, you could tell you weren't in any danger, couldn't you?*"

Thorn paused and thought about what he'd just seen. *She was right. Though the black car had approached to within 20 feet of my car, I'd sensed no danger.* He took a deep breath before realizing that she had told him there were three to go. That meant the three most dangerous—Erica, Hawke and Raven—were still at large.

"*Alec?*" she asked. "*Are you there?*"

"*Yes.*"

"*Rest up. We're not done.*"

Moments later, the phone rang.

"Hello."

"Alec, do you remember the book I told you to get at that bookstore near you?"

Thorn understood her meaning. "Yes, do you want me to pick it up?"

"Why don't you do that? I'll call you later to tell you what I want you to do with it."

Thorn realized that his role as Mr. Bait was not over and he grew somewhat tense. Maybe it was better when he didn't know people were trying to kill him. *Too late,* he thought. He had demanded that Sophie and Hunter keep him informed and they had complied.

Alec paced about the living room to dispel the tension he felt, then sat down again in the recliner and closed his eyes to gather his energy. Battle Number Two was soon to begin.

* * * * *

Thorn entered the bookstore, walked over to the New Arrivals section and began reading the jackets of books he found interesting. He wasn't sure how long it would be before his enemy would reveal him or herself, so he took his time. He forced himself to read each word, but it was difficult to concentrate under such circumstances.

After 20 minutes of not finding anything of interest and simply getting bored, Thorn walked to the magazine section at the back of the store. In the corner, he noticed a short, wiry man with a huge nose. As he looked at the man's eyes, he could sense he knew him. With one quick smile, he indeed knew it was Hunter.

Thorn moved away from him and walked slowly towards the Technology section at the far end of the store, where he began browsing the shelves. Trying to read technical books under the given circumstances was even more difficult than browsing through the new arrivals. A hint of coolness struck him. At least one of his enemies had entered the store. Nonchalantly, he turned and glanced around. The same people that he'd noted when he entered the store were in view, though not Hunter. None of his enemies were in sight, either.

He picked up another book and thumbed through it, turning in the direction he sensed an attack might come from. A whisper, a noise, a movement, anything that would serve as an excuse for him to look up, he seized, hoping to spot his potential assailant as quickly as possible.

Silently, a tall, dark-haired man with a beard, sporting tinted wire-rim glasses and wearing a corduroy sports jacket slowly worked his way towards him, all the while seeming to focus on the books along the wall.

The hair on the back of Thorn's neck stood up. This was the man. Now he had to wait until those sent to protect him identified him as well. He reminded himself not to make any sudden movements that might spook the predator. He again glanced at the man, who casually looked up. Thorn nonchalantly returned to gazing at the pages of the book he held open in his hands.

Content that his protectors had identified the man, Thorn reached up to return the book to the shelf from where he had removed it. With a single motion, the man grasped for something hidden under his sport jacket and stepped closer to Thorn. Anticipating such trouble, Thorn simultaneously took a step back and half-faced the man, feeling like a mongoose luring a cobra into danger, while remaining just out of reach of its strike.

He could not be sure, with the man's eyes covered as they were by the tinted lenses, but he presumed that this was Hawke. Thorn abruptly walked to a different section of the bookstore and glanced at a few more books, positioning himself so that he could observe him more closely. With Hawke's back to him, Thorn took the opportunity to stare at Hawke and project his thought outward, like a transmitter, to the allies gathered around him—*this* was the man.

When Hawke turned, possibly sensing that someone was watching him, Thorn decided to leave. Walking deliberately, he moved to the exit, where he watched Hawke follow him in the reflection of the store's front glass door.

Thorn exited the bookstore and walked straight to his car, parked only 10 feet away in the first row in the parking lot. While unlocking his door, he turned to see Hawke walking out the door, while pressing a keyless entry device. He heard the doors unlock on the black Chevy Blazer parked directly next to Thorn's car. But before Hawke could get into his car, two men walked quickly up to him from each side of the bookstore's exit door. Simultaneously, a van screeched to a halt directly behind Hawke's car. There was no escape.

Hunter emerged from around the corner, carrying a cigar. Thorn smiled, watching him light it up; he then gave Hunter the thumbs up sign. Smiling back at him, Hunter puffed away on his victory cigar, while his men escorted Hawke to the van.

41

You are shit in a silk stocking.
—Napoleon Bonaparte

ERICA PACED IMPATIENTLY around her workroom. Not only had Hawke failed to report in, she'd learned that her three scouts were also unaccounted for. She looked up as Raven entered. He was sweating profusely, fearing their plan might be unraveling.

"Have you heard from any of them?" she asked.

Raven shook his head, knowing that the sound of his voice became high-pitched and whiny whenever he panicked. He nodded at her to try to hide his fear.

It was too late to chalk up Hawke's disappearance to picking up some woman at a Boca singles bar. He was too disciplined not to check in. She closed her eyes and visualized Hawke, hoping to determine who could have gotten to him. After a few moments of drawing nothing but a blank, she sat down at her worktable and observed Raven, who seemed ready to cry. His frightened, helpless face annoyed her. She could tolerate him so long as he was useful, but in this state he was worthless.

"Hawke *almost* had it right. But you're not a sack of shit; you're shit in a silk stocking! Get out of here!" she yelled. His loyalty to her was no match for his recognition of a sinking ship. He stood, and without looking at her eyes, left the room quietly.

42

△△△

WHEN CAROL NOTICED Alec had not come in, she transferred his calls to her own line. She thought to herself, *It's about time he took some time off. Raising capital can sure be nerve-racking.* The phone rang, bringing her thoughts back to her job. "Carol Jordan. May I help you?"

"Oh, I'm sorry, Carol. This is Martin Welborne. I was trying to reach Alec."

"He's out this morning. He asked me to take his calls while he was gone. Is there something I can do?"

Welborne smiled, realizing he had a chance to pump Carol for information without appearing to have gone around Thorn. "Well, how *is* everything going there?"

Carol remembered Alec's words of advice as she answered, "Everything is going well. The only thing that would make it better would be if we had some more money in the bank."

"That's what I was calling about. You must be out of cash by now."

"With the employees agreeing to salary reductions in return for more stock options, we've bought ourselves at least another three weeks."

This remained a sore point for Welborne. He had checked with his lawyers and they had concurred that Thorn was well within his legal rights to grant additional stock options to exceptional employees. The fact that Thorn had classified all employees as exceptional could be questioned, but that was a matter of judgment, not of legality.

"I talked about that with Alec last week."

Carol had waited for an opportunity to mention how she hoped Welborne would be fair and consider investing again, but none had presented itself. "Martin, I think I speak for both Alec and myself when I say how pleased we are that you chose to invest in our company."

She paused to see if Welborne had a reaction. When he didn't respond, she said, "We both hope that you will consider making the company a fair offer on some interim financing."

"Alec said this?"

"He sure did." *There was no need to mention how angry he was after their meeting.*

"Well, that's what I was calling about," Welborne said. "I was thinking of lending you the $250,000, but also getting options."

"That seems reasonable," Carol said hoping to encourage him.

"With the price of these options dependent upon his obtaining additional financing."

"I think Alec would go along with that."

"Start at $2.50 a share, but have it ratchet down if he's not able to secure additional financing before this money runs out. Do you think he'd agree to those terms?"

"I think so. In fact, if you can get a term sheet over here today, I'll push for it." She hoped that Welborne would welcome the chance to have a friend on his side pushing for the deal. Alec had predicted he would.

"I'll do that," Welborne said. "But I don't want him shopping my deal, trying to get a better one from someone else. That's where he is, isn't he? Trying to raise money?"

"I believe so," she said.

"I'll give him until 5 PM to respond to my offer. If I don't get written confirmation from him that these terms are acceptable, then it's off the table. Is that clear?"

"Yes, I'm sure Alec will respond promptly," she said. "I'll get him to fax it back to you, ASAP."

Carol hung up and smiled broadly. A barely audible victory cry escaped from her lips, "Yes." She had handled the conversation within the guidelines that Alec had specified and was able to get

Welborne to act right away. Alec would be proud. She checked her watch. It was 11:55 AM. Now if she could only get in touch with Alec.

43

△ △ △

Strength does not come from physical capacity. It comes from an indomitable will.

—Mohandas Gandhi

WEARING A PAIR OF LOOSE khakis and a navy blue polo shirt, Thorn sat comfortably in his recliner, settling down to meditate. He quieted his mind and pulled in spiritual energy through the top of his head and steadily flushed it through his body.

Relaxed, he reflected on the events of the past few days. He remembered his conversation with Chapman, the investor who'd contacted him via thought projection. No check had arrived at his home. He decided to contact Chapman.

"Mr. Chapman? Can you hear me?"

"Yes."

Thorn could sense that Chapman was not as warm as in his previous communication. *Is my lack of energy affecting my perceptions?* wondered Alec silently. *"Just to let you know, Mr. Chapman, there wasn't any check in the mailroom and nothing was left with the security guard. I wanted to make sure that it's not lost."*

"No. Just have faith. It's on the way."

Thorn's stomach fluttered. *Many investors will get cold feet when it comes to writing the check. But Chapman had offered to help on his own. This could not be a case of cold feet. "You've sent it already?"*

"Not yet."

Thorn felt his pulse quicken. *"If you haven't sent it, yet, do you think you might FedEx it to me? It's important."*

"Yes, I can do that. I'll have it there first thing in the morning."

Thorn breathed a sigh of relief, realizing that his fears had been groundless. *"Thank you, Mr. Chapman. You can't imagine how grateful I am for your help."*

"God bless."

* * * * *

Thorn turned off his cell phone just before walking into Mario's Italian Restaurant a few minutes before noon, preferring to beat the rush by arriving early. The hostess smiled as she greeted him, "Hello, Mr. Thorn, right this way." Though the most desirable tables were in the outdoor courtyard, the hostess knew whenever he was alone, to seat him in a quiet area indoors with plenty of light where he could read.

Absorbed with that day's *Miami Herald*, he was interrupted by a new waiter who asked, "Iced tea?"

Thorn nodded yes, his focus on the lead story, while the waiter set down a glass of iced tea with lemon in front of him. The black and white clad waiter awkwardly recited the daily specials before Thorn selected the seafood ravioli and returned to his paper.

Thorn sipped his iced tea and glanced around the room. He absently noticed the new waiter standing in a corner watching him, not nearly as busy as the other waiters. *It's not my job to improve the efficiency of the wait staff,* Thorn thought, as he returned to his paper waiting for lunch to be served.

He ate his pasta while continuing to read the paper. The new waiter arrived with another glass of iced tea, even though his first glass was half-full. Thorn looked up and smiled at the waiter who he figured was trying to make a good impression.

Finished with the newspaper, Thorn drank the last of his first tea and took a sip from the second glass. He scanned the room for his waiter, but couldn't see him. He felt queasy and wanted his check. He watched as one of the regular waiters walked around the room with a pitcher refilling diners' glasses of iced tea.

In a moment, an overwhelming sense of knowing came to Thorn, a crystal clear perception that something was wrong. He focused on the diners in his immediate area, trying to sense if any of them represented a threat to him. He couldn't tell who they were—something was wrong with his body. He took a deep breath and attempted to flush his body with spiritual energy, but it wasn't enough.

He contacted Hunter, whom he suspected was nearby. *"I'm in Mario's."*

"I know. I'm outside."

In a flash, Thorn understood. *"They poisoned me,"* he thought. All the clues he had overlooked flooded into his mind: the new waiter who knew he drank iced tea, who watched him from the corner and who brought him another individual tea, rather than refill his glass from the community pitcher. *"You may have to come in and get me."*

"Okay, but first try to get out on your own."

Thorn stood up, not willing to wait for his check and not wanting to collapse amid potential enemies. He walked unsteadily towards the cashier as he broadcasted one single thought to the universe, *"God, please get me through this."* He forced spiritual energy into his crown and through his body to flush out the poison. He was angry, partly with himself for not recognizing the signs, but mostly with his enemies, who'd chosen such a cowardly way to kill him.

He made it to the cashier and leaned on the counter for support. The cashier regarded him quizzically and asked, "Check?" Thorn nodded "yes," unable to speak. The cashier looked at him indifferently and said, "I'll get your waiter," and left for the kitchen.

Thorn intensified his efforts to flush his body with spiritual energy. He tried to take a deep breath. Nothing. His lungs didn't work. There was no pain, he was not gasping for breath—his lungs simply were no longer connected to his body. *Is this the end?* he thought with a growing sense of panic.

But Thorn refused to die. He reached deeply in to the source of his spiritual energy and commanded his lungs to fill with air. When they were full, he stopped to let the air slowly escape through his pursed lips. He again willed his lungs to expand and then willed them to expel the used air. He continued with each breath requiring his full attention, while he leaned on the counter, sweat accumulating on his brow.

Encouraged that he could make his lungs work, Thorn forced the healing spiritual energy throughout the rest of his body. He could feel it coming into his crown stronger and stronger. He reminded himself to keep expanding his lungs to breathe. An involuntary muscle had become voluntary . . . a point which didn't matter to him, so long as he was able to breathe.

The waiter came out of the kitchen with the cashier. Staring at Thorn, the man's eyes seemed to pop out of his head, a mixture of surprise and fear. He tried to keep his distance, but the cashier ordered him to the counter. Thorn returned his stare and projected a thought directly into the waiter's head. *"Someday someone will do this to you and you'll know what it's like to feel the kiss of death."*

The waiter scribbled Thorn's order onto a check and handed it to the cashier. He hesitated to get too close to Thorn. Thorn paid for his meal and accepted his change. He was having trouble standing, but refused to show any weakness to the waiter. He let go of the counter and forced himself to balance on his own two feet. He turned to the waiter and stared into his eyes, which were aghast. Thorn handed him a dollar bill and said, "Here's your tip."

Thorn exited and walked around the corner. Out of sight of the waiter, he stopped to lean on the restaurant wall, wondering how he would make it home.

44

△ △ △

THORN MADE IT BACK to his apartment, though the energy he'd expended to walk from the restaurant to his car, drive himself home, and walk from the parking garage to his apartment door had left him completely exhausted. Needing to avoid any unnecessary activity, including talking, he decided to avoid the office until his lungs began to work normally. After kicking his shoes off and grabbing a blanket, Thorn found his way to his recliner, immediately making mental contact with Sophie and Hunter. He could sense their concern and sought to allay their fears. *"Don't worry about me—after all the fast food I've eaten, it's going to take a lot more than poison to kill me."*

Thorn sensed their sympathy, though he could also tell they were too worried to laugh at his jokes. Feeling a wave of nausea rush over him, he jumped up from the recliner and ran to the bathroom. Bending over the toilet, he tried to expel the poison, but nothing came out. Before returning to his recliner, he looked at himself in the bathroom mirror. Something in his eyes reminded him he'd been protected, somehow; that poison *does*, indeed, kill people.

Sensing his discomfort, Sophie thought, *"Don't try to do anything. Just stay comfortable and continue to bring in spiritual energy with each breath . . ."*

"You trailed off. What else did you say?" Thorn strained to hear her thoughts. Though she didn't project them forcefully, he understood her intention, *"Don't fall asleep."*

Thorn practiced not breathing to see if his lungs would work automatically. To occupy himself, he spent a few moments calculating that his lungs had expanded and contracted close to a billion times in his lifetime. Surely they had enough practice to know what to do. After several tries, they hesitantly filled with air. He said a silent prayer, *"Thank you, God."*

He relaxed, as his lungs expanded and contracted normally. He could sense that Sophie and Hunter were concerned. He mentally announced, *"I'm fine,"* and waited for their response. When none came, he decided to emphasize his point. He played the theme from *Rocky* in his mind for their benefit. *"Feeling strong now..."*

Finally, he could sense they were smiling. Hunter thought, *"Get your strength back. I'll need your help soon."*

"I'm ready to go," thought Thorn. *"This poison really pisses me off. It's one thing to try and blow me up, but if you're going to poison me—either finish the job or leave me alone. I hate feeling like I've gotta' throw up!"*

Thorn could feel Hunter laughing, as he cautioned him again, *"Just rest."*

* * * * *

It was close to 4:30 PM and Carol had still not heard from Alec, though she'd tried to call him numerous times. She walked down the hall, again, and looked into Alec's office, hoping that he'd slipped in unannounced. *No luck. Where is he?*

She walked back to her office. The terms of Welborne's faxed offer were just as he had discussed with her on the phone. He would make a $250,000 bridge loan and receive the option to purchase 100,000 shares of stock at a price of $2.50 per share. Two weeks earlier, she and Alec had expected that very same deal. The only kicker Alec had to contend with was if the company were unable to raise enough money to repay the loan within six months, Welborne had demanded that his right to purchase stock would change. In that case, he would be entitled to purchase 250,000 shares of stock at a price of $1.00 per share.

Carol reentered her office and stood holding the back of her office chair, as she glanced down at her desk and weighed the pros and cons of the offer. Alec had dismissed out-of-hand the original offer of $.50 per share. That would have given Welborne majority control of the company. With this new offer, Welborne would remain a minority shareholder, even if the company could not repay his loan and he purchased another 250,000 shares.

Walking over to a window and gazing out at the traffic below, she wondered to herself, *What would Alec do? He would bet that he could raise the cash to repay the loan. And that means Welborne would only be able to buy 100,000 shares of stock.* She pulled gently at the ends of her hair, as she contemplated possible future scenarios that might unfold from any decision her boss might make. *Alec would prefer not to be under pressure to make a deal within six months. But was that any worse than the deadline we face now?* She paused for a moment to reflect and then answered her own question out loud, "No."

"Where *is* Alec?" she added aloud. *Negotiating an even better deal, somewhere? Why hasn't he called?*

She hoped he would call soon. He would be impressed that she had guided Welborne into submitting the offer. But she worried about Welborne. *He said he'd cancel the offer if it weren't accepted by 5 PM.* She reasoned that if she asked for an extension, he would think they were using his offer as a bargaining chip with another investor—that strategy could blow the deal.

Could I accept the deal, in lieu of Alec? If he disapproved of it, he could discipline me and say I acted beyond my authority. No, Welborne would see through this tactic. He had insisted on Alec's approval.

Carol checked her watch again. It was 4:45 PM. She had 15 minutes to decide the company's future. *Should she call John Brewer, the company's attorney?* She knew what he would say. A lawyer can't recommend that you accept a deal under false pretenses.

She called all of Alec's numbers again. No answer.

Sitting down in front of her computer, Carol pulled up both the word processing program and the form that contained the company letterhead. She typed an acceptance letter:

The terms of your offer dated as of today and attached hereto are acceptable to our company. By: Alec Thorn, President.

She pulled up the fax window and went through the on-screen Rolodex that contained the destination for her fax, Martin Welborne.

She checked her watch. It was 4:55. She closed her eyes and took a deep breath. Her mouse was positioned on the Send button. She clicked her mouse and it was done.

*****

Later that evening, Carol trudged upstairs to her beachfront condo in Ft. Lauderdale, still not having heard from Alec.

Too anxious to eat, she changed into running shorts and a T-shirt and walked across the street to the beach to sit and think. Her anxiety for Thorn's personal welfare matched the anxiety she felt by her misleading response to Welborne's deadline. She guessed it was illegal to fax a letter under someone else's name. By faxing it directly from her computer, she didn't print it out and forge Thorn's signature. *Is that legal?* she wondered, somewhat anxiously.

If only I could talk to Alec. He's president and the largest stockholder. It's still his company. He should make the decision. If he chooses to reject the offer, I'll make a full confession and resign. If I'm sued, I'll plead guilty. I would never do anything to hurt Alec.

She put her head in her hands and began to cry. *Did I go too far? Have I betrayed him? Only Alec can answer that.*

It began to rain softly, but she ignored it. From the pit of her stomach, she could feel the energy draining out of her. *I've betrayed him.*

45

△ △ △

Augustus even foreknew the successful conclusion of his wars. . . . an eagle perched on Augustus' tent and defended itself vigorously against the converging attack of two ravens, bringing both down.

—Suetonius
The Twelve Caesars

SITTING IN THE DARKNESS of the safe house in Plantation, west of Ft. Lauderdale, Raven sat quietly, trying to gather his nerve. The waiter who'd delivered the poison had called earlier to tell him that Thorn had survived. Raven hesitated to contact Erica. If she found out he'd failed again, she'd be even more upset with him.

He had to do something to get back at Thorn, but recognized his adversary could not be attacked directly. Raven needed to find someone Thorn cared for deeply, but whom he would not suspect would be attacked. He reflected on the many conversations he'd taped between Thorn and his confidante, Carol Jordan, and then he had his answer. *Carol Jordan was going to commit suicide.*

He went into trance easily. He pictured her face and entered her mind. He sensed that she was upset. She wanted to speak to Thorn, but for some reason, she could not. She feared that she had betrayed him. Raven couldn't have hoped for better working conditions.

Slowly, he matched her emotions and thoughts exactly. The thoughts he planted were as if they were her own. If she recognized them as someone else's, she might snap out of her funk and escape.

"I have betrayed you, Alec," he thought. "I am not worthy of your love. I must die for you."

Raven continued repeating the thoughts in her mind. He could feel her vitality dropping, as he bled her of energy. He tried to get deeper into her mind. As he did, he saw the ocean waves rising and falling. *Carol Jordan was going to drown.*

Never pausing in his badgering her with evil thoughts, he added a new one. "I must swim as far into the ocean as I can. I must die for you."

He continued to deplete her of her vital energy. Eventually, he was certain, she would give in.

* * * * *

It was early evening when Thorn awoke from his nap. Still not feeling well enough to eat or move about, he checked his voice mail and learned of the offer from Welborne. He tried to call Carol at her condo, but got no answer.

Feeling uneasy, he closed his eyes and attempted to pinpoint what was wrong. He sensed Carol was upset and tried to picture her. He saw her sitting on the beach, crying. He focused on her with his third eye. The image that came to him was of a blackbird with its talons clawing at her brain. "Raven!" he yelled silently.

He could sense the claws release from Carol and the fear that had arisen in Raven. "It's me, Raven. Your good friend, Thorn. Aren't you happy to see me?"

Thorn could sense Raven's terror and decided to taunt him. "Whenever I say the word 'blackheart,' your blood pressure is going to rise by fifty beats per minute. If I say it too often, your heart will explode, and you'll never be able to torment another person. Am I making myself clear?"

Thorn sensed the frozen look of terror on Raven's face, as he asked, "Raven, do you have a blackheart?"

The veins alongside of Raven's pudgy face became visible in Thorn's mind, as Raven's heart beat wildly. "Maybe you didn't hear my question. I asked if you had a blackheart?"

Thorn watched, as Raven's terrified face seemed to morph into that of a true raven. In a flash, he became one and attempted to fly away. Thorn quickly leapt forward, grabbed the bird in his hand and slammed it into the rain-slicked street. The raven attempted to fly again, but its right wing was broken. *"Are you trying to run away, again, Raven? You haven't answered me. Is your heart still working? What color is your heart?"*

"Say it. Just kill me. I don't want to live!"

"Oh no, Raven," thought Thorn. *"Killing you would let you off the hook too easily. I'm going to let you live, because I want you and all your cohorts to know that if you ever try to hurt another friend of mine or any other person on this earth, I'll be back."*

Thorn gave the Raven one last kick, sending him across the street, before breaking contact and returning to Carol.

She was weak, seemingly unconscious, on the beach. He gathered spiritual energy and sent it to her from his heart and solar plexus. He would stop when her energy well filled up. Thorn was concerned, but after 10 minutes of continuous effort to fill her energy reserves, he sensed her vitality returning. He silently asked, *"Are you all right?"*

"Yes," she thought.

Thorn could sense her puzzlement. *"You had a bad experience. Don't worry. It won't happen again."*

Thorn strained to understand Carol's thoughts; they were faint and incoherent. Thoughts of deadlines and betrayals, he couldn't make out what she was thinking about. *"Don't worry. We'll talk about it later. Go home and go to sleep."*

Thorn broke contact when he sensed that she had returned home. He was relieved that nothing horrible had happened to her. He also realized that she would not remember that she had communicated with him.

46

△ △ △

For the uncontrolled there is no wisdom, nor for the un-controlled is there the power of concentration; and for him without concentration there is no peace. And for the unpeaceful, how can there be happiness?

—Bhagavad-Gita

THORN LEFT FOR HIS office at 7:15 AM, wondering about the offer Welborne had made, but most of all, he wondered what Carol would say when she saw him.

Arriving at 7:30, he noticed her car already parked outside, a half-hour earlier than usual. She was at her desk when he stopped into the kitchen, located just down the hall from her office. Unlike most occasions, she didn't get up to talk to him. Eager to check on her, Thorn walked into her office.

"I'm sorry I wasn't able to come in yesterday," he said. "I had something to take care of."

He watched as Carol looked up at him. Her eyes were not the joyous, friendly eyes that he had grown to expect, displaying instead emotions he'd never seen in her before. She was relieved, scared and embarrassed, all at once. He wanted to hold her and calm her fears, but at the same time, he could sense she was somewhat afraid of him.

After a long pause, she asked, "Couldn't you have called?"

"I wish I could have, but it was an unusual situation."

"Were you sick?"

"Sort of," he said, though not wanting to talk about being poisoned. "I'm okay." Trying to change the subject, Thorn asked, "What about the offer from Welborne?"

Carol took out the term sheet, stood up and walked around her desk as she handed it to Alec. In the message she left for him, she'd mentioned the offer and the deadline, but not the exact terms. "There's something you should know before you read it."

Thorn looked at her intently, sensing this had to do with her tortured feelings of the prior night. He nodded to her, indicating she should continue.

"I think the terms are acceptable, but I understand that as president and the largest shareholder, that's your call." She took a deep breath, but without warning began having trouble speaking. "Welborne's offer was set to expire at 5 PM yesterday. Obviously, I couldn't get in touch with you and I had to decide whether to accept on behalf of the company. I knew how much we needed the money, but at the same time, Welborne demanded that only you could accept it, not just any officer of the firm. I was caught between a rock and a hard place, and I'm afraid I did something that I'm ashamed of."

She choked out the last sentence before she started to cry. Thorn put his arms around her. "Don't worry. There's nothing you could have done that you should feel so bad about."

She tried to talk while intermittently sobbing. "I lied. I pretended to be you and faxed your acceptance of the deal. Please forgive me."

Thorn sympathized, but was not sure what to say. "Don't worry. It's okay." He hesitated to say anything else that might detract from his comforting words. "Is that it?"

She broke away from him and turned. "Yes. That's it." She avoided his eyes, trying to hide her embarrassment. She sensed that somehow he knew about her experience the night before, and quickly became defensive and uncomfortable.

Thorn tried to smooth over her awkwardness. "Whatever you did, I'm sure you did it with the best of intentions for the company *and me*, Carol. I *know* that, and I'll support you 100%, no matter what." He could sense that she had put up a barrier and did not feel his sincerity—she only heard his words.

"Well, you might as well read the term sheet," she said as she walked around to the other side of the desk. "If you want me to, I'll sign an admission of guilt and resign. If Welborne wants, he can sue me. I accept full blame for my fraud." She glanced up at Alec, her eyes betraying her pain, then quickly she turned away.

"Please, . . ." Alec wanted to tell her that she was tearing him apart, that he loved her and that she had nothing to fear. But he feared that might make things worse. "Let's not get too worked up about this. We'll figure everything out."

He looked at her, with her back still turned, and decided to leave her alone to gather her thoughts. "I'll be in my office if you need me."

* * * * *

Sitting at his desk, Thorn took the term sheet and studied it. The loan's terms were tough, but he could live with them. He might have tried to get Welborne to ease off on the price if he could not repay the loan. One dollar per share was steep, and he might have gotten him up to $1.50, but he knew that was 20–20 hindsight. Few things got him more upset than the Monday morning quarterbacks who stood around second-guessing decisions made under pressure. *Besides, the financing from Chapman would enable me to pay back part of the loan right away.*

He smiled as he put the term sheet down in front of him. *She should not be ashamed of herself. It's my fault—I'm the one who was out of touch. She was faced with a tough decision that had no single right answer. She'd felt that she had to take a calculated risk, whereas every bureaucrat in the world would have taken the easy way out. She had stuck her neck out, and that's what distinguishes a leader. Was it illegal? Probably, but her intention was honorable. It was a gutsy move.*

He paused to debate in his mind whether he should tell her right away or give her some time to gather her emotions. He stood up, preparing to return to her office and put an end to her second-guessing herself, when suddenly his phone rang.

141

"Alec Thorn," he answered.

"Well, Alec, it's too bad you decided against taking my offer, because it's withdrawn."

"What do you mean, Martin? You don't have it?"

"Obviously not."

"We faxed confirmation yesterday," Thorn said. "Are you sure you don't have it?"

"Is this some kind of ploy? I only gave you until 5 PM. This 'your check is in the mail' excuse is not going to cut it."

"No. Martin, I'm serious. We faxed it."

"Nice try, Alec. Call me if you ever get another offer that you want the board to vote on."

Thorn listened to the sound of Welborne hanging up. He walked into Carol's office. The door was open and she seemed to have regained her composure. "Carol?" he asked. "Where did you fax the acceptance from?"

"I used my computer. Why?"

"Welborne just called. He said he didn't get it."

She looked at him and seemed puzzled. She turned to her computer, while Thorn moved to look over her shoulder. She clicked on the fax icon and opened up the fax log, which had a record of all faxes sent.

4:55 PM no carrier

4:57 PM no carrier

4:59 PM no carrier

Thorn went to the back of Carol's machine and found the phone cord plugged into the back of her internal modem. He followed the cord past her desk to the corner of her office, where he found it unplugged and another phone cord plugged in that disappeared around the semi-permanent wall. Thorn yanked the cord until he heard a voice behind the wall. "Hey man, that's my computer you're pulling."

Thorn dropped the cord and walked around to the next office. One of his developers arose from his chair anticipating the question. "I was using that line to test our dialup communications program. Do you need it? Just unplug it. You almost pulled my computer off my desk!"

Thorn turned and walked back to his office. In five minutes, he had gone from wanting to praise Carol to wanting to scream at her for not confirming that the fax had been received. He decided that he should calm down before saying a word. Deep down, he realized that he was to blame.

47

△△△

LATER THAT MORNING, Thorn called the security guard at his apartment building. He recognized the voice of the man's voice, a regular there. "Hello, Stan? This is Alec Thorn."

"Yes, Mr. Thorn. How can I help you?"

"I'm expecting a package from Federal Express to arrive this morning. Have they delivered their packages yet?"

"Oh, yeah. They were here at 9:30 sharp. I have the log in front of me. I don't remember seeing one for you, but I'll check."

Thorn held his breath as the guard checked his log.

"No, sir. There's nothing here for you. Could it have come via UPS?"

"No. I was explicitly told it would be FedEx."

"Well, nothing's come in from UPS, either. Sorry."

"Thanks, Stan," said Thorn as he hung up.

He calmed himself down, by breathing deeply and expelling his anxieties through his breath. He took in some spiritual energy to flush himself, as well. And then he sought to contact Chapman.

"*Mr. Chapman? Are you there?*"

After a few seconds, Chapman established contact. "*Yes, I'm here.*"

"*I'm glad I got you. Your package has not arrived. Didn't you say it would be here this morning?*"

"*Well, there has been a slight change in plans.*"

Thorn again felt anxious, but waited for Chapman to explain what this change entailed.

"I decided that $50,000 is not enough. I have several bonds maturing later in the week. I would like to use the proceeds to buy stock in your company."

"That would be great," thought Thorn. He figured Chapman was rewarding him for his success in solving an unruly problem, rather than his business acumen. Still, it would avoid misunderstandings later if they agreed on a price per share.

"How much were you thinking of investing?"

"You mentioned $2 million in an earlier conversation. Would that be acceptable?"

"That's just what we're looking for. What about the price?"

"What would be fair?"

"Five dollars a share would place a $5 million valuation on a company poised to do $5 million in sales next year."

"That seems reasonable."

The price was less than he might have been able to get, but having institutional money in the company would be a great asset. *How soon could they close a deal?* he wondered. *"If you're planning to buy stock, could you send money for a bridge loan in the meantime?"* Thorn asked. *"Your investment will require documentation. That could take some time."*

"If we're going to do this right, I shouldn't be making a bridge loan. I'll have the papers drawn up along the terms we've just discussed and get them to you as soon as possible."

"A week?"

"Sooner, I hope. In fact, if it's not done by the end of the week, I'll send you the money for the bridge loan."

A sense of relief swept over Thorn. *"Thank you. I will work doubly hard to make sure your confidence in me is rewarded."*

"God bless."

48

△ △ △

*If I had not been born Napoleon, I would have liked to
have been born Alexander.*

—Napoleon Bonaparte

ERICA BUENAVISTA CLAPPED her hands together. *It had to be Hunter.
He was the only one who could have captured Hawke and who was
not concerned that Hawke or I would set off the bomb.* She thought
to herself, *Why couldn't those idiots at the CIA pick him up? What
kind of agency is it that they run? Don't they have anyone qualified to
handle these matters?*

She spent a few moments considering her options. *Maybe it
would be good to alert them to the presence of a fugitive—an anonymous tip. I just have to make sure they don't see me place the call, otherwise, they'll wonder why I'm calling.* She thought further, *Why
bother? If they're following me, they'll find Hunter, if he gets close.
And as long as the nuclear device goes undiscovered, the agency
wouldn't dare pick me up.*

She smiled. The federal agency charged with protecting the
national interest of the United States was going to protect *her* so
that she could extort money from both the US and other NATO
countries. That kind of logic appealed to her. *I just have to make
sure I don't lose the idiots following me.*

She walked over to an unlocked filing cabinet, began rummag-
ing around in the back of the top drawer and eventually pulled out
her favorite gun, a Walther PPK. She loaded the clip to capacity and
placed it in her purse, along with her lipstick and makeup. She
wanted to look her best when she met with Thorn for the last time.

49

△ △ △

To run away from trouble is a form of cowardice and, while it is true that the suicide braves death, he does it not for some noble object, but to escape some ill.
—Aristotle
Alexander's Tutor

THORN HAD ORDERED a cashew chicken salad sandwich from Mother's Homestyle Sandwiches and it was late arriving. He would have liked to get out of the office for a while, but he didn't want to miss any calls from prospective investors while he ate.

He got a bottle of Evian from the kitchen and returned to his office, immediately peering out the window for the deliveryman. A black Chevy Blazer approached the visitors' parking spots in front of his building.

He watched as the truck cruised by searching for a parking spot. When the truck made a left turn into a no parking zone, he saw that it was not Raven in the truck, but Erica. She wore a bright yellow shirt, probably silk. He smiled as he thought to himself, *How often in nature it is that the most dangerous animal is also the most colorful?* In this case, the image of the colorful, but poisonous coral snake came to mind.

He watched as she hesitated in her truck. *Did she plan to come upstairs to kill me or would she call to lure me to another meeting place? Maybe I should go downstairs and "accidentally" run into her. Hunter and his men would be furious. They were trying to capture her and didn't need any complications.* He elected to stay put and watch; although he also decided that, if she *did* get upstairs and asked for him, he'd meet with her.

She remained in her truck. Abruptly, she backed out and sped away. No tires screeching like Raven. *She knew how to be inconspicuous.* Seconds later, a car came roaring by. He guessed some of Hunter's men were after her. When the two vehicles drove out of sight, he sat down and closed his eyes, wanting to see what would happen, wondering if they'd get her.

He locked his mind into Hunter's, trying to be unobtrusive, but hoping that he could share what was happening. *"Am I interrupting?"* he asked.

"She saw one of my men and got spooked. If she had gotten out of the truck, we would have had her. We'll have to chase her down."

"Where are you?"

"Going north on A1A."

"Are you going to be able to box her in?"

"I don't have enough men. I had to use two cars to get rid of the agency guys who were following her."

"Aren't those guys on our side?"

"It's complicated. You'd think so, but we couldn't have them around."

Thorn could sense that Hunter was yelling at his driver or into a phone, or both. *"We've got her cornered. She tried to get across the Linton Boulevard Bridge and it just went up. She tried to turn around, but one of my men has her boxed in."*

Thorn tuned into Hunter to understand what was happening. He sensed pain in his hand. She was shooting at Hunter and his men. Thorn stopped asking questions and silently prayed that no one would get hurt.

Thorn was awakened from his meditation by a knock on his door. He jumped up to see the deliveryman with his sandwich. Thorn paid him and went back to Hunter. He sensed a lull in the action and decided to venture a question. *"What's happening?"*

"She seems to be out of ammunition—her gun only holds seven rounds. I don't think she planned to get into a firefight. But we're not going in until we're sure she hasn't reloaded."

"Would it help if I told her to stop?"

Thorn sensed Hunter smile. *"You think she'll listen to you?"*

"*We'll see.*" Thorn focused his attention on Erica, while letting Hunter tune in. "*Erica. Oh, Er-i-ca.*" Thorn stretched out his thoughts like he was calling Lassie on TV. He stopped when he sensed that he had her attention. "*It's me. The man you love to hate.*" Thorn could sense her surprise. "*Surprised? Did you think you and your friends were the only ones who could communicate like this?*"

"*Go to hell, Thorn.*"

"*Why are you so angry? I thought we were going to have lunch next door at the Chinese restaurant when I saw you pull up. I must say you looked pretty in your yellow blouse.*" He could tell he had her full attention. "*You knew they weren't going to let you just walk up here without checking for weapons, didn't you?*" he asked. "*That's why you don't get a knife and fork at a Chinese restaurant. It's not polite to have weapons at the table. You don't want to insult the cook. You can't show up at a Chinese meal and take out a gun. The chef would be offended.*"

"*Shut up.*"

"*I can tell you're not in a good mood. Come back and we'll—*"

"*I said shut the hell up!*" Her thoughts, filled with anger, exploded in Thorn's head. "*Tell these men that I'm going to set off the bomb unless they back off!*"

"*They don't care.*" Thorn kept his thought matter-of-fact. "*Listen. You haven't killed anyone yet. You don't want to make things worse. You kill one of them and you'll have to kill them all, because they won't stop until you're dead. Just throw down your weapon and give up.*"

She hadn't yelled at Thorn yet, so he figured he might be making progress. He tried hard to lock onto her emotions, to understand what she was feeling.

Soon, he felt the sense of failure, that even if she got out, she knew everything was hopelessly screwed up. Years of work down the drain. With all of it seemingly lost, she questioned whether she should fight it out to the end.

Thorn decided to project his thoughts again. "*It's not worth it to give up your life for no reason. Start over. Maybe you can make up for some of the damage you've done.*"

149

Thorn paused to see if his comments were having any effect. He decided to try a new tack. *"If you try to fight your way out, it would be the same as committing suicide. You'll just come back and go through the same thing again.*

"If you think this life was hard, I can't imagine what your next life will be like. That's going to be an even worse nightmare," Thorn thought.

Thorn could sense her desire for closeness. She was alone. The big cheese that now stood alone. He projected his thoughts again. *"It's not too late to start repairing the damage. Today is the first day of the rest of your life."* He wasn't sure what he was saying or if it made sense, but he knew that making sense wasn't really all that important at the moment. She just wanted someone who would talk to her.

"Just give up," Thorn thought and waited.

Hunter cut in, *"We have her in custody. She's handcuffed and locked in our van. My men will clean up the site. Congratulations."*

"Did anyone get hurt?"

"No one got killed," Hunter thought.

"How's your hand?"

Thorn could sense Hunter smiling at Thorn's perceptive question. *"It's nothing really, barely a scratch."*

Thorn smiled. No one had gotten hurt and Hunter was laughing again. *"Was that your real nose I saw the other day in the bookstore?"*

"Why?"

"Well if it was, it's no wonder she shot you."

Hunter's laughter drowned out his reply.

50

△△△

*I amused myself with reading seriously Plato's Republic.
. . .While wading thro' the whimsies, the puerilities, and
unintelligible jargon of this work, I laid it down often to
ask myself how it could have been that the world should
have so long consented to give reputation to such nonsense
as this?*

—Thomas Jefferson

A GLANCE AT THE company's bank statement online reminded Thorn that he needed money. He remembered that Chapman had still not sent any correspondence. He sat down in his desk chair to meditate. *"Mr. Chapman? Are you there?"*

Within a few minutes, he sensed Chapman connect with him. *"Yes, I'm here."*

"I just wanted to check that everything is still moving forward."

Chapman did not respond, which made Thorn pause. If Chapman were going to renege on the deal, he would not have acknowledged Thorn's contact. He waited.

"You think you deserve this investment?" Chapman asked.

"You mean does the company merit such an investment? Yes, definitely. I expect that with this capital, we'll be doing $20 million in sales within 3 years. The return will be outstanding and the products we sell will help the world."

*"I mean you. Do **you** deserve this investment?"*

"I'm not sure I'm following you. This money is not for me. For me, it represents a chance to build a solid company, but it's not going into my pocket."

"So you think you deserve it?"

Thorn stopped to think. *Is this some sort of trick question? Chapman explicitly said he was trying to get the terrorists to stop. He had also said he was impressed with what I had done. Sure I deserve it.* He answered, *"Yes."*

"You're sure?"

Thorn continued with his thoughts. *What is the value of capturing terrorists? What is a human life worth? Have I earned the opportunity as a result of my actions? Definitely. "I accomplished everything you said you were trying to achieve,"* Thorn thought. *"By that criterion, the answer is definitely yes."*

"You seem very confident."

"I am," he thought. He reasoned that Chapman was testing him. Most investors want to be reassured that their investment is going to be fruitful. Often they will try to gauge the confidence of the company leader. If he's not confident, they won't invest.

"Don't you know that pride is a sin?"

"What are you talking about?" Was Chapman joking? No. He could sense Chapman's feelings—he was dead serious.

"You need to learn humility. Until you do, you will get nothing," Chapman thought.

Thorn was numb. *Was this a bad joke? Was he testing me?* Thorn fought to maintain his composure. *What was it that Chapman wanted? "I don't understand. How can you say I need to learn humility?"*

"Just what I said."

"Why? Have I acted in some unseemly way? Have I boasted about my actions? No one knows what I've done. Even if I wanted to tell, who would believe me? I acted exactly as I wish someone else would have acted in my place. What more could anyone ask for?"

"I have made my decision."

Thorn fought to control his emotions. *Had Chapman deliberately sought to lead me on to dash my hopes, for no apparent reason? That didn't make sense. Was I mistaken? Had I misinterpreted Chapman when he had promised $50,000 and then $2 million? No, because then he wouldn't be talking about this humility foolishness. This had nothing to do with business or my actions.*

Slowly Thorn's confusion turned to anger. He broke off communication before he said something he might later regret.

* * * * *

Thorn was still disturbed by the deceit of the man who pretended to be a man of God. He needed advice. After a few deep breaths, he sought his mentor. *"Sophie? Can you hear me?"*

"Yes."

"You're aware of my conversation with Chapman?"

"Yes."

"What's wrong with him?"

In her silence, Sophie made clear her desire to avoid getting in the middle of the dispute.

"Can't you say anything?"

"Everything will be all right. Let me get back to work."

"Wait. I'm not asking you to betray a trust. I need to know if I was wrong. If so, I'll apologize and put it behind me. Tell me if I misinterpreted what he said. Did he promise me funding?"

"Yes."

"Then why is he reneging?"

"He thinks he's helping you."

"I need this kind of help? I need him to judge me as to whether I'm too proud?" he asked. *"How long has he decided that he is God?"*

"You ask me questions that I cannot answer."

"That you can't or that you won't?"

"Both."

"Tell me. Is this new? Was he always like this? How did he get to be so influential? Doesn't everybody recognize him for what he is?"

"Let me go back to work. Just meditate on your questions."

"Is he holding a gun to your head?"

"Contact me later."

Thorn sat up, feeling more disgusted than before. He realized that he should be thankful to Chapman—he had taught him something new. *A liar is a liar, no matter how you communicate.*

51

△△△

That's my trade. Hatred. It takes you a long way further than any other emotion.

—Paul Joseph Goebbels
Nazi Minister of Propaganda

RAVEN SAT ALONE in a corner at Ft. Lauderdale airport, waiting for the plane to arrive that would take him on the first leg of his journey. His right arm was broken and his ribs were taped. The small propeller aircraft was late, which he had grown to expect. *It was typical of all the backward Caribbean companies that provided such flights.*

He could not be sure what would happen to Erica, but prudence dictated that he retrieve the documents from their secret hiding place on Haiti. The documents contained incriminating evidence against a host of leaders in the western world. If he had to, he would trade these documents for his freedom. Only he and Erica knew of their location and he couldn't take the chance that she might reveal the location before he got there.

Raven reflected on the events of the past few days. He fervently wished that Erica would reward his obvious talent by sharing power with him—ideally through marriage. He understood her offer to Thorn was made for political reasons, but it was still an insult to him. But all this paled in comparison to her rejection of him earlier that morning.

He checked his watch—it was nearly 2 PM. The eight-hour time zone difference meant it would be nighttime at his original mentor's headquarters. Raven went into trance and attempted to contact the one who had taught him how to focus and manipulate hatred. Within seconds, the Cleric responded.

"Yes, my student. You have not contacted me for some time."

"I didn't want to risk having her find out that I might be serving another master."

"Where is my package?"

"I don't know. Only Hawke and she knows and neither of them would tell me."

"Why wouldn't she sell it to me?"

"I don't know. She just changed her mind. She never consulted me."

The explanation satisfied the Cleric, though he sensed Raven was merely hedging his bets. *"What can you tell me?"*

"We've had a lot of trouble keeping this man Thorn under control."

The Cleric had observed Raven's failures through Raven's own eyes. He could sense that Thorn's ability was growing every day, but he was not concerned. *Raven is not my best student. Though he shows some promise, he has not mastered the ability to hate totally and without mercy. That is why he has lost his battles to the idealist, Thorn.*

"Hawke's been captured," Raven thought. *"And Erica may be next."*

"Where is she?"

"I think she's going to try to kill Thorn herself. That's why I'm afraid she may be captured."

"Hm-mm-m." The Cleric hid his true reaction from Raven. *Without Buenavista,* he secretly thought, *I will have to rely on Gecko to find my package. And the time is swiftly approaching for my most talented student to take his rightful place at the head of the organization I have so painstakingly put together.*

"Keep me informed," thought the Cleric, turning his attention back to Thorn.

155

52

△ △ △

Things are not always what they seem.
—Phaedrus

WHILE MEDITATING THAT evening, Thorn tried to contact Sophie. *"Sophie? Are you around?"* he asked.

After a minute or so he received her response. *"I'm kind of busy. Can you contact me later?"*

"Sure. Can I help you with anything?"

"I'm collecting pollen that is only released once a year from a very rare plant. There's nothing you can help with."

Thorn attempted to view what she was doing through her eyes. He figured she would tell him if he were in the way. He sensed she was in a dense tropical jungle. The air was warm and humid. *"Are you at home? Is this your garden at home?"*

"No. These plants only grow on Haiti."

"What are you doing gardening this late at night?"

"I have no choice. When the plant decides it's time, it's time."

"What's this pollen used for?" He sensed that his questions were not bothersome.

"How many questions—"

"Raven!" He interrupted Sophie when the image of the evil man appeared to him. He tried to sense where it came from. His picture of Sophie in the tropical forest turned black.

He hesitated to contact her, not wanting to distract her. He sent her energy, hoping it would help, and waited for her to reconnect with him. After a few minutes, he sensed Sophie return.

"Are you all right? What happened?"

"*It was Raven. He must have followed me.*"

"*What happened? Did he attack you?*"

"*He tried.*"

Thorn smiled. He sensed that not only had the attack failed, but also that Sophie had put him in his place. "*What did you do to him?*"

"*He's limping off into the woods. He went flying when he tried to jump me,*" she thought. "*Best of all, the plant I've been tending has opened and the pollen is releasing.*"

Thorn laughed partly at her understatement and partly in admiration, as he thought, "*Appearances can be deceiving.*"

53

△△△

Three things cannot be long hidden: the sun, the moon, and the truth.

—Buddha

THREE DAYS LATER, Gecko returned to NATO Headquarters in Brussels. The mood was much more tense than the previous meeting, as everyone now knew that the terrorists Buenavista, Hawke and Raven were missing.

The foreign ministers and secretaries of each of the NATO countries were in attendance. The Secretary General opened the meeting. "Gentlemen, as you know the extortionists have disappeared. However, we believe they've been captured."

"Why suppose that?" asked the German Defense Minister. "Maybe they're just hiding."

"They haven't responded to our requests for how and where to transfer funds. Even if they chose to remain out of sight, they would answer us."

"My government objects to negotiating with terrorists," said the British Secretary.

"I understand. We have not given up trying to find the nuclear device. We still hope to recover it, but time is running out. The original deadline expires in only five days."

"Maybe they're bluffing," said the Englishman.

"Do you really want to find out?" asked the Secretary General. He turned to Gecko. "Can you update us on the search?"

Gecko rose to address the group. "We are focusing our efforts on the oilfields near the Caspian Sea, which intelligence indicates is the most likely target. Otherwise, I'm afraid we're no closer to uncovering the device's location than we were three days ago. We are pursuing all leads."

"How did these terrorists get captured from under the noses of the FBI and CIA?" asked the Englishman.

"I'm sorry. I can't answer that," Gecko replied.

"Can't or won't? You're holding something back. How can we make a reasoned decision without good information?" demanded the German.

"He's right," said the French Defense Minister. "We're all in this together, so we need to pool our information,"

Gecko guessed Hunter had captured them. *No one else has both the ability and the motivation,* he reasoned. "Gentlemen, it's possible that whoever has them may contact us. This could help us locate the device. I suggest we wait a few more days."

The room was silent. There was no other alternative.

* * * * *

Thorn was finishing his dinner—two slices of pizza he'd wolfed down at the Cannoli Kitchen—when he sensed that someone was trying to contact him. He recognized it was Chapman, as he established contact.

"*Do you think you've learned your lesson?*" Chapman asked.

"*About pride and humility?*"

"*That's right.*"

"*I thought about it.*"

"*And what did you conclude?*"

"*I believe a man should be judged by his actions,*" Thorn thought.

"*You have not learned your lesson. You are still prideful.*"

Thorn avoided saying anything to incite the financier. "*Have you asked anyone else's opinion?*" Thorn asked.

"*I don't have to.*"

Thorn felt sickened by the man's hypocrisy. *Would Chapman be satisfied with anything less than total subservience? No,* Thorn thought, *he'd just find another excuse to avoid keeping his word.*

"You call me prideful while I seek advice from others. You're the one who never considers he might be wrong."

"You need to learn humility," Chapman thought.

"So you're going to renege on our agreement?"

"You bring this all upon yourself by your refusal to learn your lesson."

Thorn shook his head. *"You have no compassion whatsoever for the common man. I wish I could take solace knowing that some-day you will experience exactly what you're doing to me,"* Thorn thought. *"But knowing you will suffer gives me no pleasure."*

"Until you learn your lesson, it's you who will suffer. It's for your own good."

Thorn responded angrily, *"Who are you to judge me?"* He paused to wait for a response. Chapman's silence caused his anger to grow. *"I'm proud of what I did. Is that what you mean?"* Thorn raised the amplitude of his thoughts. He was no longer just communicating with Chapman, but broadcasting his thoughts to all who could hear. *"Let all the universe know. I'm proud of what I did. I thank God that I was given the gifts I needed to succeed. And if I could do it all over again, I would do it all exactly as I did. If this is a sin, then I am guilty. Strike me dead."*

"Your words prove I am right about your pride," Chapman thought.

Thorn drew in a slow, deep breath and watched his anger subside, feeling a wave of spiritual energy pass through him. *"You complain about the speck in my eye and neglect the plank that is in your own."*

"Blasphemer!" shouted Chapman silently. *"Now you claim to be God? You know nothing of God or humility. Surely you will go to hell!"*

Thorn was surprised at the vehemence of Chapman's response —he could perceive his flushed face and quivering arms, with hands knotted into fists. *"Chapman, I don't know what you're talking about, but I do know there is only one God and you're not Him."* Thorn shut off further communication with the hypocrite.

54

△ △ △

RAVEN HAD REGAINED his poise after the humbling events of the past few days. *Thorn certainly surprised me when I was busy with Carol. And if I hadn't been injured by Thorn, I know I would have taken care of Thorn's mentor. I am not a coward.*

Luckily for him, he was free. Although Erica still rejected his attempts to contact her, she'd acknowledged that she had been captured.

He sensed someone demanded to communicate with him, so he quickly entered trance. He recognized the thoughts of his teacher. *"What is happening?"* asked the Cleric.

"Everything is falling apart," Raven thought. *"She's been captured and I couldn't retrieve the documents that we had hidden."*

The Cleric knew of Raven's beatings. *"You must redeem yourself for your failures."*

Raven's pulse quickened. *"Ask and I will do your bidding."*

"Thorn must not interfere with the final initiation of my student. I want you to keep him occupied."

Raven's heart raced. He hoped to avoid a direct confrontation, which would be painful. *"How?"*

"I am sending three students to kill Thorn. Brief them and use your energy to augment their hatred. Failure is not an option."

The Cleric broke contact, leaving Raven shivering in a pool of cold sweat.

* * * * *

Gecko left the meeting and returned to his hotel. Using a secure line, he called Luis Vega, Director of Latin American Operations for the CIA.

"Vega, this is Gecko."

"Yes, sir," said Vega. "How may I be of service?"

"Any new leads on Rivera's murder?" asked Gecko, referring to the ex-CIA station chief of Colombia.

"Nothing," said Vega. "El Diablo is still the prime suspect, but we can't find him."

"Try looking in Boca Raton."

"Florida?" asked Vega, surprised.

"That's right."

"I'll get a team there today," said Vega, knowing that Gecko's information was usually good.

"I want to be the first to know of any new developments."

"Understood."

Gecko hung up. *Ideally, Vega's team will pick up Hunter and I'll get to Buenavista before NATO. Even if Vega's men don't pick up Hunter, they'll make it more difficult for Hunter to operate freely.*

After changing his clothes, Gecko took a cab to the shopping district, checked to make sure he was not followed, and then took another cab to a safe house outside the city. Inside, he opened a hidden compartment in the bedroom closet and took out the secure computer with an attached satellite phone.

Gecko logged on to retrieve messages, eager to see if White had pinpointed and transmitted the location of the package. He found White's encrypted message waiting for him. Quickly he decoded it and had the coordinates he needed.

Taking out a compact disc from his jacket pocket, he inserted it into the CD drive. His PAD encrypted transmission would be mathematically unbreakable.

He punched in the code number of the receiving unit. When he heard the connection complete, he said, "Pegasus-6, this is Alpha-6. Do you read me? Over."

"Roger. Please authorize, over."

"Authorization code charlie oscar bravo romeo alpha. Over."

"Authorization confirmed. Over."

"The encrypted coordinates in question are being downloaded to you while we speak. Use your company to sanitize and secure a perimeter one-klick in diameter centered on these coordinates. Over."

"Roger," said the Pegasus company commander.

"Nothing. I repeat. Nothing is to enter that space without my authorization. Over."

"Roger."

"Over and out."

Gecko knew the order would never be traceable to him. It didn't matter. If anything went wrong, no one would be around to complain.

He needed to pass the coordinates on to the Cleric, but had to wait for the Cleric to initiate contact. He checked his watch. He would be contacted within 48 hours. The match was lit.

55

△ △ △

Resistance to tyranny is obedience to God.
—Thomas Jefferson

ERICA BUENAVISTA SAT in the small, windowless room, waiting for her captors. The only evidence of them was the food tray they pushed through a narrow slit in the door while she slept. She spotted video cameras mounted in each of the four corners of her room, eliminating her privacy. She had no choice but to meditate to seek answers to her questions.

She suspected Raven was still free, but didn't bother to contact him. *That coward can't be counted on,* she thought angrily. *Maybe in a few days, he might regain his nerve, but I doubt it. He is despicable.*

Before long she felt a sensation in the middle of her forehead. She could not identify the person. "*Who are you?*" Erica thought.

"*You were probably too young to remember me, but I knew General Buenavista and your mother.*"

"*You were also in the government?*"

"*I handled investments for the government and later, for many of the top military leaders. Many of them realized, even before the Falklands fiasco, that their wealth and position were unstable. They wanted their money out of the country and invested safely.*"

"*Why are you contacting me?*"

"*There are some funds of the General's that are legally yours, now that both he and your mother are gone.*"

"*How much?*"

He laughed. "*You're still preoccupied with money, aren't you?*"

"What do you mean?"

"Do you remember when you learned to walk? You were only a year old. I held up a gold coin and you walked across the room to claim it. When I put the coin back in my pocket, you cried so long and so loud that I had to give it to you."

"My mother told me that story. You were the man holding the coin?"

"Yes."

"What is your name?"

"Rune Chapman."

The name meant nothing to Erica. *"I never expected that my father would leave anything for me. And the fact that I didn't know of any money means you didn't ever have to contact me. Why did you?"*

"I knew your mother. I am interested in your well-being."

"If you want to help me, get me out of here. I'm locked up. Or didn't you know that?"

"I'm making some discreet inquiries to find out where you're being held. The government's not involved. At least, not yet."

Erica paused to think. *He knows too much not to be aware of the nuclear device. This is not an occasion where the big lie would be better than a small lie. Better to confess a few items and pretend full disclosure and hope he reveals everything. "I might be guilty of a few other things, as well,"* she thought aloud.

"You mean the nuclear device?"

"Yes."

"No one is about to come forward and admit they knew anything about that."

Erica smiled. Maybe she could get out of this mess and start again. *"It's going to explode if I don't get out."*

"Where is it?" he asked.

"Somewhere in Pakistan. I don't have the exact coordinates. Only my associate knows exactly."

"Hawke?"

"Yes," she thought. *"How did you know?"*

"Never mind. Where did this fixation on Thorn start?"

"He humiliated me."

"When?"

"2,000 years ago."

"When you lived as Cleopatra?"

"Yes."

"I understand you recently suggested he marry you. Was that what you really wanted or was it part of your getting back at him?"

"If it didn't work out, I would have terminated the relationship." She smiled at her clever use of ambiguity.

"Do you still want him to marry you?"

"He's already refused. He's an idealist—he can't be bribed."

"I see. I'll check back with you later. God bless."

* * * * *

Thorn sat at his office desk, reviewing cash flow projections. Feeling a sudden tingling sensation in the middle of his forehead, he altered his focus to establish contact. He was shocked to learn that it was Chapman, but waited for Chapman to proceed.

"I bet you could use some money," thought Chapman.

Thorn remained silent, as he fought to maintain his composure, not allowing himself to be provoked.

"Have you learned your lesson yet?"

Thorn took several deep breaths and thought to himself, *Am I obligated to my shareholders and employees to make a deal, if it would help the company? No one would know that I even had such an option, if I chose not to disclose it.* But Thorn did not let his ability to hide this option affect his decision. He decided it would be based on the truth, not just on what was revealed.

Despite the narrow latitude that he allowed himself, he had come to his conclusion. *No, I will not make a deal with this hypocrite. To do so would be to reward evil. Resistance to tyranny is obedience to God.*

"Do you hear me?" Chapman asked.

"I hear you."

"Well, what's your answer?"

With his mind's eye, Thorn could see the hypocrite in his study, reclining in his favorite chair, his shocking white hair the only feature distinguishing him from millions of other businessmen or academics.

"You think of yourself as a philosopher-king, but you're just a petty tyrant." Thorn could sense the arrogance pouring out of the man who believed that only men like him, the truly enlightened and learned, were fit to rule.

"Then don't be surprised if some of your employees decide to work for people who can afford to pay them," responded Chapman in a mocking tone.

Thorn erupted with rage. He saw himself in Chapman's study, standing over the little man, who paused momentarily, before bolting from his chair to cower in the corner against his bookshelves, his eyes bulging with fear.

"I could break you in two at any moment I choose," Thorn thought. *"Try bothering any of my employees and see how patient I am."* Thorn returned to his body.

Back at his office desk, Thorn took a deep breath and attempted to regain his balance. His contact with Chapman broken, he sensed he was being watched.

A voice spoke, *"You did the right thing."*

Thorn could sense the presence of joy and approval about his actions. He tried to pinpoint the source of this joy. He gasped as an image formed in his mind—an image of the one who had taught the world to love your enemies. Thorn cried openly with both joy and sorrow. *"I am trying to live as you instructed, but it's not easy. He mocks me and cares nothing for the common man. He's only interested in increasing his own power."*

"Don't worry. What happened was very important. He has revealed his true intentions. And so have you."

"I was ready to crush him."

"He attempted to provoke you, but you refrained from violence."

"There is hope for me?"

Laughter filled Thorn's heart and soul. He felt at peace.

* * * * *

Once again, Thorn focused on the company's need for capital. He suspected Chapman's promises were too good to be true. He was glad he hadn't told anyone of this potential deal, preferring to wait until it was in hand before presenting it. He knew that he had other options and now he needed them.

Thorn grabbed the folder for Tachyon Communications and opened it up. He noted that his contact, Johnson, should have already returned from his vacation. He picked up the phone and dialed the direct line to his office.

"Johnson, here."

"Hello, Bill. It's Alec Thorn."

"Oh, hello, Alec. I'm glad you called. We were just discussing your company."

"You were?"

"Yes. Our president, Brent Hall, wants to meet with you. He'll be in Miami tomorrow night and will stay through the following afternoon. Can you meet that morning before he flies out?"

"Of course," he said. "How close are we to a deal?"

"Off the record?"

"Sure."

"I got the go ahead to draft a formal offer, subject to the President's approval after he meets you."

"Great," he said. "Can you give me an idea of the terms?"

"Don't quote me," he said, "but it's going to be for the same amount that we discussed a few weeks ago, but at the low end of the price range."

Thorn figured that translated into at least $2.50 per share. He could live with that, even more so with Chapman reneging and the Welborne deal coming apart.

"How soon can you get it to me?"

"Not until after you meet the president. It's just a formality, but I have to wait. Whatever you do, don't spit in his eye."

Thorn laughed and hung up, his tension melting away, as a feeling of relief swept through his body.

56

△ △ △

THORN LAY IN BED. He decided it was too early to get up. He quieted his mind and filled his body with spiritual energy. He sensed that Sophie was there to check in on him, that she was smiling with pride at her student.

"*Don't you ever sleep?*" he asked.

"*There'll be plenty of time for that later,*" she thought.

"*Have Hunter's men found Raven yet?*"

"*No.*"

"*One thing I don't understand. How can someone bring themselves to kill an innocent person without remorse?*"

"*Why don't you ask him?*"

"*He's not going to cooperate with me.*"

"*Try him. He understands spiritual power.*"

Thorn focused on Raven. He perceived him in bed, his right arm in a cast and his ribs heavily bandaged. He projected his thoughts, "*Raven, I need to ask you a few questions.*"

Thorn could picture Raven's eyes filling with fear, hoping the voice inside his head would go away.

"*I'm talking to you Raven,*" Thorn thought.

Raven brought his arms alongside his head, as if to protect himself from being pummeled. "*Please, leave me alone,*" he thought. "*I have nothing to do with it.*"

"*With what?*"

Raven paused to consider whether Thorn was playing with him or unaware of the assassins. Fearing that Thorn could travel at will into and throughout his mind, and having tasted the bitterness of doing battle with Thorn already, he decided he'd better not try to hide anything and risk angering him again.

"Listen, I'm telling you, now, that his men are already on their way to kill you."

"What men?"

"Three assassins. The Cleric sent them—not me."

"Who's he?"

"He's the head of a cult that teaches how to use and manipulate hatred. He's the one who taught us the power of hate. It takes you a long way further than any other emotion."

Thorn felt sick. *"Tell me more about this Cleric."*

"A number of years ago, the Cleric recognized the great spiritual power of a particular young boy and wanted him to himself. So, he killed the boy's parents and proceeded to raise him. It will shatter the young man's personality when he finds out."

"What do you mean?"

"The boy is an innocent young man. He loves his stepfather and doesn't know what he's done. When he finds out, he'll develop an alternate identity, a totally distinct personality. The Cleric will control him."

"How?"

"Certain key phrases will trigger him to assume the alternate identity. At that point, the Cleric will transfer all of his hatred to him. He will assume this new identity and the change will be irreversible. The Cleric's goal is to have the young man become evil incarnate."

Thorn sensed that Raven sincerely believed what he was saying and noticed an air of resignation, not defiance or deception, accompanying his thoughts.

Raven thought, *"I tell you this, Thorn, because I'm already a dead man. They'll be coming after me right after they kill you."*

Thorn broke contact with Raven and focused on Sophie. *"How could anyone do such a thing?"* he asked.

"Not everyone has emotions," she thought. *"Crocodiles eat their young."*

* * * * *

Thorn got dressed, jumped in his car and arrived at his office in less than an hour. While reviewing his email and voice messages, he sensed that someone was trying to contact him.

"Your visitors are on the way," thought Sophie.

Thorn took a deep breath. *"The ones that Raven said were coming?"*

"Yes."

"Okay. Here we go." Thorn leaned back in his chair and put his feet up on his desk. He breathed deeply and pulled in additional spiritual energy through his crown chakra. He focused his attention on the emissaries of hate who the Cleric had sent. He perceived the three men clearly, leaving Ft. Lauderdale airport in a rented car and driving up A1A to his office.

He put himself into their minds and realized that they were just following orders. They had been taught to hate, just like Raven. They also had learned to fear the Cleric. He established contact with all three simultaneously. *"My spiritual brothers. I've been waiting for you."*

Thorn sensed some surprise, but their discipline covered up any fear they might have shown. *"We have been warned about your trickery. You cannot fool us as you did Raven,"* thought the one in the front passenger seat.

He's apparently the leader of the hit squad, reasoned Thorn. *"Why is it you want to kill me? Have I harmed you in some way?"* Thorn asked.

"The Cleric has decided it. It is not for us to question his teachings."

"Do you always follow his orders blindly?"

"He speaks directly to God. We are mere students."

"You rely on him to tell you God's will? Didn't Muhammad teach you to pray to God five times a day?"

"God is powerful. Like our master."

"Do you not wish for your brother that which you wish for yourselves?" Thorn gave the thoughts substance, not knowing where they came from.

"Do not try to deceive us. We will find you and kill you."

Thorn understood power was all they valued. *"Do not bother looking for me. Here I am."* With a thought he was sitting in the back seat of their car, next to one of the assassins.

The assassin in back screamed. The driver turned to look at Thorn and drove off A1A into a large, coconut palm on the side of the road. Thorn could sense the look of fear on all three of their faces.

"We did not know that you were so powerful. Please do not hurt us."

"Why do you think the Cleric has sent you to kill me?"

"We do not know."

"Does he fear to meet me himself?" Thorn asked.

He knew that, at the moment, this trio would agree to anything to get away. He made them a proposal. *"As God is just and merciful, so shall I be. If your master does not fear me, tell him to come to me directly. I do not wish to deal with anyone but him."* Thorn paused to let his message sink in. *"Is that clear?"*

"Yes," the three answered in unison, as they pressed themselves against the car doors, hoping to place as much distance between them and Thorn as possible.

With a thought, Thorn left them, as he returned to his body.

57

△ △ △

To overcome evil with good is good, to resist evil by evil is evil.

—Mohammed

THE NEXT MORNING, Thorn sat at his office desk, attempting to sketch an outline of an investor presentation, but unable to concentrate. Instead, he pondered the identity of the mysterious Cleric, whom the assassins both revered and feared. Deciding he wanted to find him, he put his notes away, relaxed his body and went into a deep meditation.

In his mind, he was in a mansion somewhere in Central Asia, but which country wasn't clear to him. Thorn moved from room to room throughout the lavish, sprawling home, searching for some activity. Eventually, he came upon a darkened room with its door partially open. Thorn slipped in. Immediately to his left, was a man wearing a hooded robe, kneeling in front of a black candle. Focusing in on this sinister figure, who he *knew* to be the Cleric, he moved cautiously into the room to get a closer look. A feeling of coldness came over Thorn. Sensing his proximity, the Cleric slowly turned his head toward Thorn. Though the hood of the robe left his face in shadow, Thorn could sense the presence of evil.

As he stood in front of the Cleric, who appeared at least 70 years old, Thorn stared into his eyes, but saw nothing but darkness. He could sense hatred, not merely for any one person, but for all of humanity. Thorn reacted without thinking, *"You are no match for me or my associates."*

The man's eyes showed no fear, but Thorn detected a glimmer of surprise, though hidden by his careful manner. Without blinking or moving, he responded to Thorn's boast, *"We'll see."* Slowly he turned back towards the candle.

Thorn opened his eyes and returned to his office. Feeling sick to his stomach, he flushed his body with spiritual energy. As soon as he recovered, he closed his eyes again to understand his experience.

Hoping for more information, he was presented with another scene, that of a young man playing in a garden with children. The man was obscured by what seemed like dense smog. Thorn was puzzled that smog followed him as he moved among the children.

Thorn guessed he was seeing an aura filled with hatred and negativity. Somehow this young man was tied in with the evil, bearded Cleric in the mansion. The young man sensed Thorn's presence, but made no attempt either to communicate with or avoid him.

Thorn again opened his eyes and returned to the physical world. He wanted to rest, but his intuition told him to go back. So, once more, he shut his eyes and went deep within himself.

Slowly the picture came to him; both the Cleric and the young man from the garden were together in the mansion. He sensed anxiety in the Cleric and innocence in the young man, who Thorn intuited was the stepson Raven had mentioned. The entire scene was filled with negativity. He remembered Raven's words, and soon an odd thought struck him—the Cleric wanted to die at the hand of his stepson.

Thorn locked onto their thoughts. The Cleric's words were powerful and clear. "Funding promised to our people was denied by the infidels. You must take action and avenge this betrayal."

Thorn sensed that these were trigger phrases that he had programmed into his stepson, words which would automatically elicit hatred.

The Cleric said, "Evil must be punished."

"Yes, Father."

"Your parents were murdered. The evil must be avenged."

"I will avenge them," said the young man, his pain at losing his parents compounding the hatred already within him. "Death to the infidels."

"Death to the *killers*," the Cleric said, emphasizing his correction.

"Killers?" asked the young man. "Were they not infidels?"

"No."

"You know who killed my parents?" he asked, now quivering with hatred. "Tell me!" he screamed. "Tell me and I will kill them!"

"I killed them," said the Cleric, matter-of-factly.

Thorn could sense confusion in the young man. "Father, tell me who killed my parents."

"I killed them," he repeated.

Thorn sensed the confusion turn to shock and disbelief. "No," he whispered, looking into the Cleric's eyes. He loved his stepfather. It was not possible.

The Cleric stared into his stepson's eyes with black, emotionless eyes. Thorn could feel the complete lack of emotion in the Cleric. Slowly, the stepson came to realize that the Cleric was not lying.

The young man's feelings of shock slipped into total despair. Thorn felt them in his own body. The emptiness in his stomach. The blackness of his thoughts. The overwhelming desire to deny the truth.

He both loved and hated him. But, which was it? Thorn could feel the man's thoughts polarize, like an amoeba ready to split into two separate cells. He had to stop it.

Thorn took in as much spiritual energy as he could to flush away the overwhelming sense of hopelessness. He felt the young man's sadness as if it were his own emotion. Thorn's face twisted into convoluted expressions of pain, and he began crying together with the young man at the pointlessness of his parents' murder. The young man's sadness felt more painful than any emotion Thorn had ever felt.

Soon, the feelings of hopelessness waned, as betrayal and hatred began filling the void. Thorn could sense the Cleric staring at his stepson, his dark, steely eyes now filled with hate. The Cleric did not apologize or try to lessen his son's pain, instead, he relished the agony that he put his stepson through. The feelings of hatred in the young man built upon themselves, escalating rapidly. At that moment, the Cleric began psychically pouring his own storehouse of hatred into his stepson, as though he were using a funnel to fill a bottle with poison.

Thorn tried to draw away the feelings of hatred from the young man and channel spiritual energy through his own body to flush out the evil thoughts. He could sense that the hatred was growing faster than he could funnel it away. Thorn felt himself engulfed in hatred, a vortex of evil. He was becoming consumed, overwhelmed by the hatred—and then, unexpectedly, he felt a new power surging up within himself.

Completely out of nowhere arose a feeling of pure bliss. Unconditional, absolute, infinite, divine love quickly filled his entire being. Without questioning where it came from, Thorn felt this sacred current rush through him and into the young man, swiftly purging him of his hatred, just as a sudden burst of sunlight chases away the darkness.

Thorn paused to catch his breath. Suddenly, just as he relaxed, he sensed a dark cloud pass over the stepson. His deeply engrained programming had kicked in again and his thoughts immediately reverted back to the need for revenge. Though Thorn was astonished, he realized there was no time for reasoning.

He psychically grabbed the young man to prevent him from killing his mentor, while continuing to funnel this universal love through his body. Now, he had succeeded in angering both of them: the young man, because he had prevented him from exacting revenge, and the Cleric, because he had prevented the splitting of his stepson's personality.

His intervention turned the attention of both of them to Thorn. The spell was broken. The young man turned to his stepfather, looked directly in his eyes, and without emotion simply said, "Leave." Thorn sensed the Cleric still wanted his son to kill him, rather than simply send him away, but said nothing. He shot a quick glance at Thorn, but again said nothing. Thorn watched the Cleric slowly shuffle away. The young man's eyes were downcast. Thorn left him alone with his grief, but with his personality intact. As he departed, Thorn wondered to himself, *How long will this last?*

58

△ △ △

All that is needed for the forces of evil to triumph is for enough good men to do nothing.
—Edmond Burke

THORN SAT AT A table in the Boca Diner, sipping an iced tea and working on his presentation for the president of Tachyon. Outside in the parking lot, a Ford Taurus pulled in and a short, wiry man got out. He peered into the windows of the diner and smiled when Thorn made eye contact. Thorn recognized him as Hunter, but he no longer had the same huge nose.

He entered and approached Thorn's table. "Do you mind if I sit down?" he asked, before proceeding to sit down.

"Are you here to save my life again?" Thorn asked.

Hunter laughed and replied "No, that shouldn't be necessary. Your two loving admirers are locked away and Raven is hiding out," he said. "Let me know if you see any terrorists, though."

Thorn laughed. His mood became serious when he noticed the bandage on the man's left hand. "I didn't mean to be disrespectful the other day when I made that crack about her shooting you," Thorn said.

"No offense taken. That's how I can tell if a person has an aptitude for this line of work. If you can make jokes while people are trying to kill you, you're not likely to freeze up."

"I didn't have time to freeze up," Thorn said. "Everything happened so fast, I just reacted."

Hunter smiled. "It's called being in the moment. People can do amazing things when they forget about the past and future." He looked into Thorn's eyes. "Even so, I've seen trained agents crack under similar circumstances."

He sensed Hunter's sincerity and was grateful to hear from someone who knew what he had been through. "Thanks," Thorn said. "It was pretty hard, but not as hard as raising capital for a new company."

Hunter laughed. "Being that this work is so easy, maybe you could help with one last thing."

"Sure. What is it?"

"No one has located the nuclear device, yet," Hunter said. "I was hoping that if you were to mentally lock onto Hawke, you could tell me exactly where it's located."

"I already did that. It's in Pakistan at the base of two twin peaks. I could draw you a picture, if you want."

"No. I need you to come with me," said Hunter.

"To Pakistan?"

"Yeah."

The absurdity of this request struck him. His first trip ever out of the country and he's going to Pakistan to disarm a nuclear bomb. "I can't go with you," Thorn said, half laughing.

Hunter remained silent.

"I'm not qualified—I'm an entrepreneur, not a secret agent or some nuclear expert. My company's future depends on my being at a meeting tomorrow morning." Thorn paused. "For a minute, I thought you were serious."

Hunter continued to regard Thorn without saying a word. Thorn returned his gaze and could see what appeared to be hurt in his eyes. He blinked and looked again, but it disappeared.

Thorn looked down at his presentation. *No doubt, it will impress Tachyon's president—cutting edge technology applied in an innovative manner. The world will have faster communications and my employees and I will make a lot of money. This is what I've dreamed about almost every night for two solid years. I'm on the threshold of realizing it.*

Thorn looked up to explain that to Hunter. Once again, he saw a subtle sign of hurt in Hunter's eyes, not readily apparent, but clear enough to Thorn. And then the absurdity of flying to Pakistan began to make sense. Getting rich didn't seem important, at the moment. A chance to save the lives of millions of people was. "When would we have to leave?"

"Right now."

59

△ △ △

THORN WAITED OUTSIDE the hangar on a small private airfield in the Everglades. With no city lights and overcast skies, it was pitch black outside. Hunter explained that it would be better if Thorn waited outside while he got things ready. Thorn decided to check in with Sophie.

"Sophie. It's me. Are you there?"

"Yes."

Thorn could sense a smile on her face. *"I figured I should check in and tell you what I'm doing."*

"I already know."

"How?"

"Hunter asked me about it before he went to meet you."

"So you approve?"

"Yes. There's no other option."

"I'm flying halfway around the world with someone I just met. Granted he did save my life, but shouldn't I be nervous?"

"Don't worry. Your personalities are similar."

Thorn watched as Hunter walked out of the hangar and waved for him to come in. *"Here he comes. I'll keep in touch."*

"Follow me," Hunter said. "It's dark in here."

Thorn followed right behind Hunter, unable to see much of anything. "Climb up this ladder and sit in the seat behind me." Thorn groped his way up and felt his way onto the seat. Hunter secured the canopy over them. Thorn couldn't see anything other than the dull greenish lights that barely illuminated the cockpit interior.

"I can't see anything. How can you see what you're doing?" he asked.

"Don't worry," Hunter said. "Ready?"

"I guess so."

The plane slowly taxied out the hangar door and onto the barely lit runway. "Hold on," Hunter said. The plane raced down the short runway and lifted almost straight up into the sky.

"What kind of a plane is this?" Thorn asked. "All I see is black."

"It's a kind of stealth fighter, but has a few extra features. It's similar to the B-4 bomber, but smaller."

"You mean the *B-2* bomber."

"No. B-4 represents the current state-of-the-art. It's got a quantum drive. That means we won't have to refuel. It also lets you hover."

"How did you get it?"

"I test piloted some of the craft out at Groom Lake—you know, Area 51? Certain parties sympathetic to the cause lent it to me."

"The government?"

"Not exactly."

"Is this plane stolen?" Thorn asked, feeling more than a little alarm at the notion. "What happens if we get caught?"

"Relax, they can't see us on radar."

After a few minutes, Hunter broke the silence. "You'd better get some rest."

"Oh, don't worry about me," said Thorn, "this is very relaxing. I'm flying in a stolen plane into a hostile environment to look for a nuclear bomb. Why shouldn't I be relaxed?"

Hunter turned to Thorn. The greenish glow of the panel revealed the hint of a smile on Hunter's face. "You still think raising capital is harder than this?"

Thorn closed his eyes and tried to get some sleep.

* * * * *

Thorn stirred. "Where are we?" he asked, not wanting to open his eyes. "How long have I been asleep?"

"We're approaching a Soviet military base on Novaya Zemlya near the Arctic Circle. I've made arrangements to land. You've been out for about 6 hours."

181

Hunter landed the craft without incident. Hunter and Thorn climbed down from the cockpit, and, immediately, armed guards escorted the two of them into a small office. Inside loomed the large, imposing figure of a Russian military officer. Thorn could not determine the man's rank or even what branch of the military he represented, but the man's body language hinted at his power.

The men spoke to each other in a language that Thorn assumed was Russian. After exchanging greetings, they embraced. Clearly, these men had a long history with each other. Switching to English, the Russian asked, "Who is he?"

"He's my navigator," Hunter said.

The explanation seemed to satisfy the Russian. He gestured to a frail-looking man, who was standing next to an electronic device not much bigger than a microwave oven. "Yuri will brief you on what needs to be done."

Thorn watched as Yuri demonstrated and explained to Hunter how to disassemble and disarm the nuclear device. At the heart of it hung a baseball-sized sphere of metal, which Hunter placed in a small lead box.

Thorn caught Hunter's eye. "Is that thing safe?"

"It can't explode, if that's what you mean," he said. "It's not fissile—it's made of depleted uranium." He smiled. "It may come in handy." He pointed to a duffel bag and said, "Carry that out. We're leaving."

"Good luck, my friend," said the Russian. "If you come back, I'll break out the Stolichnaya and we'll drink a toast."

Thorn could not be sure if he meant "if you return" or "if you survive." And, at the moment, he didn't want to know.

60

△ △ △

CAROL TRIED TO WORK, but her anxiety made it impossible to concentrate. For the second time in a week, Alec had disappeared without any warning. His meeting with the president of Tachyon was in less than one hour. She grabbed at the phone when it rang. "Carol Jordan, may I help you."

"Carol, this is Bill Johnson from Tachyon. I was trying to get Alec and got transferred over to you," he said. Carol remained silent, not sure how to respond. *How do I explain that Alec's gone AWOL?*

"It's just as well," said Johnson. Carol remained silent, as Johnson continued, "I'm a little embarrassed, but we're going to have to postpone the meeting with Alec. The president had to return last night.

Carol sighed. Alec was off the hook, but the company was still without capital. "Can we reschedule?"

"We'll both be down on the 10th. Can we make it for the next morning, say 9 AM?"

"That should be fine."

"As part of our due diligence, we would like to have your technical people meet with ours to discuss compatibility issues," Johnson said.

"Will they be coming also?" she asked.

"No. We felt it would be better if they came to our offices on Water Street. We're just a few blocks from the Network Access Point, where we'll be interfacing our equipment."

"I'll bring our lead developer and senior systems analyst with me," said Carol, knowing Alec would want a businessperson to accompany the technical staff.

"Super. Our head of development will be expecting you and your staff."

"And I'll have Alec call if there's a problem at this end," she said as she hung up, still not sure if she should be angry or worried.

* * * * *

Gecko returned to the safe house on the outskirts of Brussels hoping for a message on his secure computer from the Cleric. After establishing his identity he decoded and read the message:

Call me.
—The Cleric

He inserted the compact disc into the satellite phone and pressed the codes that would provide him with a new one-time PAD. His authorization complete, he dialed the number. Thirty seconds later, he heard the Cleric's voice at the other end.

"Where's my package?"

"The coordinates are being downloaded as we speak. The area has been secured."

"Good. I'll send a team to pick it up."

"Yes, sir."

"The candle will burn extra bright."

61

△△△

It is easier to denature plutonium than to denature the evil spirit of man.

—Albert Einstein

HUNTER'S VOICE interrupted Thorn's thoughts. "Okay, we're in Pakistan and getting close to where I think the nuclear device must be. I want you to focus on the picture you have in your mind of Hawke planting it."

Sitting behind Hunter in the cockpit of the stealth fighter, Thorn closed his eyes and stilled his mind. He locked onto the picture easily. "Okay. I have it."

"Before you open your eyes, I want you to picture the horizon. Make a note of the mountains. Tell me which direction Hawke came from. Most likely, Kazakhstan, but we can't be sure."

"All right, I can see it clearly. We're looking for twin peaks. Then a depression in the mountains, like I told you before."

"Okay. Open your eyes and look out the front window."

Thorn opened his eyes slowly, trying to retain the picture in his mind's eye, while he made sense of what was coming in through his normal vision. "Nothing looks familiar," he declared.

"We're not close enough," Hunter said. He quickly pressed a series of buttons on the instrument panel in front of him. "Watch the monitor. How about now?"

"Those might be the two mountains."

Hunter pressed another button to zoom in.

"Yes. Those are the twin peaks. I'm sure of it."

"Then we'll be there in 15 minutes."

A red light lit up on the instrument panel and Hunter's brow furrowed momentarily. "We're being pinged," he said.

"What does that mean?" asked Thorn.

"Radar."

"Isn't that common?"

"In the middle of the desert—not likely," Hunter replied. "Someone's looking for bogies and they've got some pretty sophisticated equipment."

"We're invisible to radar, though, aren't we?"

"Yeah. And now we'll see whether this warp field works."

"What's that?" asked Thorn.

"It generates an electromagnetic field that warps light so that it bends around us. Anyone looking at us will actually see what's behind us."

"You've seen this work before?"

"The secret service uses it."

"What?"

"Do you remember watching when President Reagan got shot? How many men do you remember were surrounding him?"

"Close to a dozen."

"Well, there are just as many guarding the President today. You just don't see them, because some are using cigarette pack-sized devices that create tiny warp fields."

Thorn looked at Hunter, wondering if he was putting him on.

Hunter said, "The funny thing is that the field doesn't fool dogs. They can see right through it and will bark like crazy. That's why the Secret Service hates dogs."

Thorn shook his head as if to clear it. As they got closer, they could see men and equipment, most notably black helicopters, encircling the twin peaks. Hunter spoke, "They're not Special Forces—that's CIA black ops."

"Maybe they're looking for the bomb," said Thorn.

"You see anyone searching for anything?" Hunter asked. "They don't have any idea what they're guarding."

"Why not tell them?" Thorn asked matter-of-factly. "It's *their* butts that'll be saved."

"You don't know the mindset. They don't do anything without orders. They've been specially selected and trained to give up their lives, if that will result in the success of the mission."

"What do we do?" Thorn asked, forcing himself to focus on the problem and not the fear that wanted to surface.

"I think I can land without them identifying us. Let's find the bomb first, then worry about it."

"Okay," he answered mechanically, then took a deep breath to center himself.

"I'm going to circle around once to locate the area with the least amount of troops. Let's hope they don't hear us."

Thorn closed his eyes and took another deep breath. Hunter interrupted him. "Oh, shit."

Thorn opened his eyes to see Hunter pointing to the west. In the distance, he could see a convoy of vehicles approaching the area.

"Toyota Land Cruisers," Hunter said. "They're coming this way. We'll have to hurry. We have two hours at the most."

Thorn felt his stomach contract, as he continued to breathe deeply.

Hunter brought the craft down about 100 yards from the front of the twin peaks, still undetected.

"Put on the suit," said Hunter, as he unloaded the duffel bags, "but carry the hat. I want you to find the depression you viewed in your mind."

Thorn closed his eyes to freshen the mental image of Hawke with the device. He opened his eyes and stared straight ahead. Puzzled, he said, "It doesn't make sense. The mountains match exactly, but there's no depression. It's solid rock."

Hunter was busy with the Geiger counter, "I get a bit of radiation straight ahead, but it could be background noise. Where did you say the depression was?"

"Straight ahead."

"Tell you what I want you to do," Hunter said. "I'm going to take your arm. Close your eyes and start walking. Use your inner sight. Walk fast, because once we're out of the plane, we'll be visible."

Thorn walked straight ahead as he envisioned the scene in his mind's eye. Suspicious of Hunter's plan, he opened his eyes and stopped a few feet from a solid rock wall.

"What are you doing?" asked Hunter. "Just shut your eyes and keep on going."

"But it's solid rock!"

"Just do it." Thorn realized Hunter was dead serious.

Thorn closed his eyes again and walked on, this time with his free arm outstretched in front of him. He kept reaching forward, expecting to feel the rock, when he felt his feet go out from under him—Hunter dropped the duffel bag he was carrying to grab him with his other hand.

"Yow," said Thorn, opening his eyes. "It's a long way down."

Hunter pulled him back. Thorn pushed his hand through the solid rock in front of him. It tickled.

"I thought this might be the case. It's a holographic projection to hide the cave entrance." Hunter was kneeling down, as he peered into the "rock."

Thorn chuckled. "It looks like your head is embedded in the rock."

Hunter pulled his head out. "There's a ladder over there." He pointed to the right. As Hunter stepped over to it and then began his descent, Thorn followed right behind him.

A satellite dish lay in the depression, with cabling that disappeared into a cave opening. With any luck, it would lead to the bomb. "You wait here," said Hunter. "I'll be back." Before Thorn could protest or say a word, Hunter turned on the lantern and entered the cave.

Thorn climbed up on a large rock and looked out towards the rocky desert. Even though the sun was overhead, it seemed much brighter outside the depression. The plane they'd flown in was fully hidden from view, and suddenly, Thorn felt slightly wobbly in the knees. *Is this real,* he wondered? He shook his head to remind himself of where he was and what he was doing.

Thorn closed his eyes and tried to perceive what Hunter was doing. He sensed that Hunter had descended a few feet down a narrow path, before the path forked. Following the cable through the right fork and proceeding down another hundred feet, Hunter finally had stopped. The picture of an electronic device, just like the one back in Russia, appeared in Thorn's mind.

He opened his eyes again. The surreal nature of the situation disappeared, and he realized that, indeed, they really *were* trying to disarm a nuclear device. Thorn closed his eyes again—this time to pray. *Surely God would watch over a man trying to disarm a nuclear bomb, but it wouldn't hurt to ask for help.*

He could sense some sort of contact with the crown of his head, but could not make out any images or hear any words. He hoped his prayers would be answered.

Feeling antsy to *do* something, Thorn explored the walls of the depression. A small black box lay in an indentation in the wall. He knelt down and pulled it out of the wall to get a better look. As if a light was switched on, the entire area became engulfed in bright sunlight.

"Damn," whispered Thorn, intuiting that the holographic field was down. He looked around and found a cord that had come loose. He plugged it back in and the bright sunlight disappeared. Thorn wondered, *Should I tell Hunter? No, he's got enough to worry about. Besides, no one's looking for the device, anyway—it's doubtful anyone saw it.* Sitting himself down a large rock, he decided to simply wait for Hunter.

62

△ △ △

WHITE WAS ANALYZING images at his computer when he was notified of the anomaly. He had programmed the system to automatically scan for anything unusual within five kilometers of the coordinates he had previously given to Gecko. Two bodies suddenly appeared near the mountain.

He blew up the satellite image and viewed it in real time. The two figures began moving slowly towards the mountain, then disappeared. White quickly changed frequencies, scanning from low infrared to ultraviolet, but he'd lost them. Suddenly, part of the mountain disappeared and a large depression formed. Twenty seconds later, the mountain appeared whole again.

He zoomed out to gain a wider perspective and could see the black ops troops with their helicopters and equipment surrounding the perimeter. He zoomed out farther and saw a convoy of trucks approaching from the west. Judging by their speed, he estimated they were less than an hour away. Tiny beads of sweat formed on his brow.

White's mind raced. *What's worse? To have Carson killed by Gecko's men or be court-martialed for deliberately hiding evidence? How can I explain this to my boss? It was classified above top-secret —eyes-only, according to Gecko. He must have greater authority than my boss. But I have no proof that I've ever even met Gecko. Black ops would never publicize their operation. They didn't exist officially. But who was in the convoy? Did Gecko know? In for a penny, in for a pound, I guess.* White decided to maintain the information blackout, though he knew he was taking a grave risk. Realizing his call might be monitored, he dialed the number Gecko had given him, and recited the agreed upon code, "Two guests are crashing the party."

That would give Gecko his heads up. It was the best he could do. He turned back to the monitor and continued to watch.

* * * * *

Gecko was just returning to the safe house from NATO headquarters when his cell phone rang. He took it out and noted the caller ID. White had left a message. He dialed the appropriate codes and listened. Two intruders were at the site. He took out the satellite phone and activated the encryption device.

"Pegasus-6 this is Alpha-6. Do you read me? Over."

The curt, disciplined voice of the company commander responded, "Roger. Please authorize, over."

"Authorization code tango charlie romeo alpha bravo. Over."

After a slight pause, a reply came through, "Authorization confirmed. Over."

"Perimeter has been breached. Two intruders. Dispatch unit to the center of your position. Sanitize the area. Repeat. Sanitize the area. No exceptions. Over."

"Roger," said the commander.

Gecko put down the satellite phone and mused, *This will be the last time Hunter will interfere.*

63

△ △ △

I'm a great believer in luck and I find the harder I work, the more I have of it.

—Thomas Jefferson

THORN HEARD THE whir of chopper blades, a low, rhythmic pulse that, at first, seemed far away. He climbed on top of a rock formation and saw a sleek, black helicopter, like a deadly flying insect, approaching rapidly. Thorn's pulse quickened and his chest tightened, as he crouched low atop the sandstone boulder. Suddenly, he realized they didn't see him—that is, they *couldn't* see him. He slowly stood upright and forced himself to breathe deeply, calming his mind.

No need to warn Hunter, Thorn thought. *He'll hear the chopper as soon as he comes out of the cave—even though it does seem much quieter than the military helicopters that occasionally fly down the coast past my apartment.* Thorn watched the chopper land only 300 yards from where the Stealth fighter lay hidden. Men in full battle gear poured out with weapons drawn. *Hunter was right,* he thought. *They weren't looking for a bomb—they were looking for intruders.* Thorn took another deep breath and reminded himself, *They can't see me.*

Hunter exited from the cave carrying the small lead box that previously had held the uranium ball.

He motioned to Thorn to come down and step into the cave. "They just get here?" he whispered, aware of the nearby commotion. With the chopper engine running, there was no danger of their being overheard.

"Yeah," Thorn said. "I'm afraid I may be to blame—I accidentally turned the holographic field off before turning it on again. I didn't think they saw me, though."

Hunter nodded. "They didn't—but the NSA satellites overhead did." Hunter looked with some concern at Thorn, then began quickly and methodically running through his options. He removed his Glock from his shoulder holster and checked that the gun was loaded to capacity. "We need to get out of here before the others come—otherwise we'll never get out."

"By *shooting* them?" Thorn asked, "Why not make a deal instead?"

"What do you suggest?"

"Let's give them the disarmed nuclear device. They get to be heroes and we get to leave."

"That would make sense if this was a business deal, but these guys aren't businessmen. They're not interested in being heroes or making money. They're just interested in following orders . . . which means kill on sight."

Thorn's body shivered involuntarily. He forced himself to concentrate on his intellect, rather than focus on his emotions. "You've got a better plan?"

"Unfortunately, no. Firing at them will draw too much attention." Hunter exhaled. "All right, we'll try your plan. I'll have to get one of them in here to negotiate." He looked at Thorn. "I'm going to grab the guy giving the orders into his headset and throw him down here. You grab his sidearm and stay out of his reach. He'll know more ways to kill you laying on his back than you can imagine."

Thorn had no time to think before Hunter climbed up the ladder and made a clicking noise. The leader immediately turned in his direction and began cautiously walking closer. In an instant, Hunter emerged from the solid rock to grab the leader's rifle and yank him backwards into the pit. The leader swung his arms out and caught Hunter in the throat before landing heavily on the ground, with his helmet jarred loose. Thorn grabbed the gun out of the man's holster, as Hunter jumped down and clamped a chokehold on the dazed leader before he could respond.

Thorn could see that Hunter couldn't talk. He could feel his thoughts, however, and listened to what he was thinking. *"Don't tell him any more than he needs to know."*

Thorn nodded to Hunter. He spoke aloud to the commander, while making sure to emphasize his words by projecting his thoughts directly into the man's mind. "Inside the cave behind us is a nuclear device. It's set to explode in less than one hour. Whoever sent you here intended for you to die." Thorn paused to let the message sink in.

"We are willing to make a deal. You can have the nuclear device. You get to recover it and be a hero. We get to leave. No one is to know we were ever here." Thorn peered into the leader's eyes to see if he understood. "Nod your head if you understand."

The commander nodded, his weather-beaten face showing no sign of emotion.

"Tell your men to get in the chopper and return to your previous position. Use your headset. If you refuse, we will *kill* you and shoot your men one-by-one from behind this holographic cover."

Hunter let up on his chokehold. The leader took a deep breath, then shouted, "Intruder alert! Mountain base—"

Hunter tightened his grip to end the communication, but the damage had been done. He could feel Hunter's thoughts. And then he heard Hunter's voice, now a hoarse whisper, "They know we're here and they don't care about dying. They're already coming for us."

64

△ △ △

WHITE CONTINUED TO peer at his computer screen, as one of the black ops men suddenly vanished into the mountain, just like the two men before him. Pulling back to a broader view, he could see that the convoy was less than 30 minutes away.

He zoomed in on the convoy. Toyota Land Cruisers. "Holy shit!" White gasped. He picked up the cell phone and dialed Gecko's code number again. When he got the prompt to leave a message, he said, "More guests are coming to dinner. The party will start in 30 minutes." He held his breath and hoped to God that no one would ever find out what he had done.

* * * * *

Gecko took out the satellite phone and activated the encryption device as soon as he received White's warning. "Pegasus-6 this is Alpha-6. Do you read me? Over."

The headset on the unconscious soldier buzzed. Hunter pulled it off of him and held it where all three of them could listen.

"Copy," answered Hunter.

"Pegasus-6 this is Alpha-6. Do you read me? Over."

"Roger. Authorization please. Over."

"Authorization code tango charlie romeo alpha bravo. Over."

Hunter hesitated a split second before responding in his hoarse whisper, "Confirmed. Over."

"Status of intruders? Over."

"Area secure," said Hunter.

"Excellent. Convoy approaching from the west. Open west perimeter and let them enter secure area. Pull back and avoid detection. Over."

"Roger that. Over."

"Over and out."

Hunter immediately turned to the commander. "You heard that," he snarled. "If you follow *these* orders, you'll get to live. If not, you *won't* get a second chance."

Thorn watched the commander's eyes and sensed the conflict in his mind. Should he order his troops to pull back or to sanitize the area? He projected his thoughts directly into the man. *"Follow orders. Pull back. Follow orders. Pull back."* Thorn repeated his thoughts continuously while the man considered his alternatives. The commander nodded his head.

Hunter said, "Tell your men to pull back, *now.*"

He relaxed his chokehold and let the commander speak into the headset.

"Convoy approaching from the west. Open west perimeter and let them enter secure area. Avoid detection. Centaur squad, return to perimeter, repeat, return to perimeter. I will stay behind until further notice." Hunter tightened his grip to indicate the communication was over.

Thorn and Hunter watched as the men obediently followed the leader's orders and filled the chopper. The chopper lifted off and disappeared.

Hunter's voice returned. "Look back there," he said, pointing to the cave opening. Without warning, he used his sidearm to bash the commander across the back of his head, crumpling him to the ground.

"Was that necessary?" asked Thorn.

"We can't let him see us in the Stealth fighter. Don't worry. He's not hurt too badly."

Hunter grabbed the headset from the unconscious leader and picked up the lead box. "Let's go."

"We can't leave this guy here," said Thorn.

"Why not?" asked Hunter, incredulous at Thorn's comment. "This is the same guy that wanted to *kill* you."

"You heard the orders, Hunter, they're supposed to avoid detection. If the next group finds him, they'll be suspicious."

Looking down at the man, then out across the open plain in front of them, Hunter begrudgingly agreed, "Okay, let's get him out to the plane. We'll dump him once we're past the perimeter. But first, unplug the holographic projection device."

Thorn pulled the power cord and the two men dragged the commander up the ladder and dropped him on the ground. Hunter turned to Thorn and said, "Since it was your idea, you carry him."

Thorn picked up the man in a fireman's carry and walked alongside Hunter, who carried the lead box containing the fissile plutonium core. As they neared the area where the plane had landed, Hunter said, "If you look carefully, you can see the edges of the warp field. It's a little easier if you don't look directly at it, but instead use your peripheral vision." Staring almost 90 degrees away from the area where the plane was parked, Thorn could barely make out subtle distortions in the field's boundary.

Thorn stowed the lead box and the unconscious man behind his seat, while Hunter prepared the Stealth for take off. Minutes later, with Hunter at the controls, they quickly climbed into the sky. Landing again about a half mile east of the perimeter, Hunter turned to Thorn and ordered, "Drop your buddy overboard. And hurry up."

Holding onto his shirt collar, Thorn lowered the unconscious man as far as he could before dropping him on the ground below. As soon as they were back aloft, Hunter circled back to see the convoy of trucks pulling up to the now visible nuclear site.

"They won't be happy when they find out there's no fissile material in the bomb," said Thorn.

"They won't be able to tell without taking the core apart and analyzing it. More than likely, they won't know until it's too late," said Hunter, with a knowing smile.

65

△△△

The strong are good, only the weak are wicked.
—Napoleon Bonaparte

CHAPMAN SAT IN HIS recliner, deep in trance, seeking to communicate with Erica. After a few unsuccessful attempts, he established contact. *"Erica?"*

"Yes, I'm here." She hesitated to make contact, half expecting to hear news of a nuclear explosion.

"Are you okay?"

"Yes. I'm fine," Erica thought.

"There haven't been any nuclear explosions, if that's what you were wondering," thought Chapman, anticipating her question.

Erica remained silent, knowing it should have exploded.

"NATO suspects you were bluffing. My sources tell me Hunter was involved, with help from Thorn and the Russians."

Erica winced. *Thorn, again.* She clenched her teeth and stared at the gray wall directly in front of her, as her outrage slowly left her. Regaining her composure, she thought, *"You said you were interested in my welfare. Why?"*

"I told you I knew your mother."

"So did thousands of other people. Why did you wait so long before coming forward? My father has been dead for years."

"Your father's not dead."

Erica grew suspect. *"He's dead. I was there. I saw him die."*

"You mean the General?" teased Chapman.

"Who else? Are you playing games with me?" she demanded.

"*What happened?*" Chapman asked innocently, partly diffusing her rising anger.

"*It was reported in all the papers,*" she replied. "*The peasants attacked our house. My mother was killed, as well.*"

"*Your mother was killed by the General.*"

Erica's mind froze. Aside from her parents, she was the only one at the house when her mother was killed. Her father had been drinking and he had killed her mother after she confronted him about his blatant taking of mistresses. But no one else knew this. "*Where did you get that idea?*" she asked suspiciously.

"*The bullet that killed your mother came from the General's gun. He had powder burns on his hand. He shot your mother.*"

"*Why didn't this come out in the investigation?*" she asked hoping to draw Chapman out.

"*It wouldn't have looked good if one of the heroes of the republic had killed his wife. Besides, he died at the same time, so they decided to kill two birds with one stone.*" Chapman paused. "*They still haven't found the General's killer. Do you have any idea what happened?*"

"*I have no idea.*"

"*They found the gun. It had fingerprints on it. The fingerprints were yours.*"

Erica clenched her teeth, enraged that she had been found out. *But no one has accused me of anything. Why hasn't anyone come forward?*

Chapman sensed that she would not admit her act. "*Don't worry. I took care of the evidence. You're clear. But tell me—why did you do it? Were you protecting your mother?*"

"*Yes,*" Erica replied quickly. "*I loved her.*" She chose not to reveal the real reason she had killed him, reflecting back to how he struck her mother all the time. Reviewing the past violence within her mind's eye, she could see that her mother was simply weak. *The strong are good, only the weak are wicked,* she mused to herself. *If he hadn't struck me he'd still be alive.* Erica could sense Chapman's sadness. "*You seem to know everything that happened, then. Why do you say that my father's not dead?*"

"*Because I am your father.*"

"*What?!*" she blurted out, responding with a measure of disbelief and intrigue.

"*Your mother and I were in love, Erica. The General didn't love her. She was beautiful, tall and blond—he only wanted to parade your mother around as a trophy. Haven't you ever wondered why you have blond hair when the General's was jet black?*"

Erica sensed that Chapman was vulnerable. "*Well, Father, how about getting me out of here?*"

"*I can't do anything until you're located. No one has even acknowledged that they have you.*"

"*Hunter's responsible. You know that.*"

"*Yes. I expect he'll turn you over to the U.S. government very shortly. No one will want any embarrassing revelations to come out in a public trial. Once they take possession, I'll get them to release you into my custody.*"

"*You can't do anything before then?*" she pleaded.

"*I'll make some inquiries,*" he offered.

"*Thanks,*" she answered, content that she had pushed him as far as she could.

"*God bless.*"

66

△△△

Blood is thicker than water.

—Anonymous

WHILE THORN TRIED to rest in the back seat of the Stealth cockpit, a sudden tingling sensation in his forehead signaled that someone was trying to telepathically contact him. He quickly entered into a receptive mode and was surprised to learn it was Chapman. *"What do you want, Chapman?"* he asked, not masking his scornful sentiments.

Ignoring Thorn's tone, he replied, *"I'm glad I was able to get you. I was afraid that you might still be angry at me."*

"Why would I be angry at you?" Thorn asked, openly incredulous. *"Just because you're a lying hypocrite who makes promises he never intends to keep?"*

"I've been thinking a lot about what has happened over the past few weeks," thought Chapman, disregarding Thorn's insult. *"I realize that I might have been hard on you, but I hope you realize that I did it for your own good."*

"I need this kind of help about as much as I need to contract leprosy."

"I had to see for myself whether you could handle the strain of such pressure," thought Chapman.

"How does financial pressure compare to having people poisoning you or trying to blow you to pieces?" Thorn sensed that Chapman would readily lie to advance his own agenda. *"What is it you want, Chapman?"*

"I am hoping that you would consider joining our family."

"What?"

"*I would like you to consider marrying my daughter. She would make a great wife.*"

"*You cannot sell your daughter like a piece of property. It's her decision to make.*" He remembered Erica's ideas on marriage and thought, *Both she and Chapman think alike. Is this a coincidence?*

"*Of course it would require her approval, but I'm sure she'll agree,*" Chapman thought.

Thorn paused to consider Chapman's motivation. *Was this the offer of a man who thought he could buy his way out of any difficulty, or an honest attempt at reconciliation, no matter how repugnant?*

Before Thorn could respond, Chapman thought, "*As soon as you're married, I'll set you up with $20 million.*"

Thoughts exploded from Thorn, "*You know nothing about me or who I am! Did you think that if you couldn't ruin my life, you could just buy it?*"

Thorn quieted his thoughts and tried to sense Chapman's feelings. There was no emotion. To him, it was a simple business deal, certainly no reason to get excited. Thorn shook his head, as he broke contact with Chapman, wondering what the daughter of such a man would be like.

67

△△△

To err is human; to forgive, divine.
—Alexander Pope

WHITE STUDIED THE satellite images. The troops surrounding the perimeter of the site were disbanding and the convoy of trucks was packed up and heading south to Karachi.

He breathed deeply. In a few more minutes, he would reengage the live feed to the official satellite reconnaissance record and no evidence would exist of the events in the Pakistan desert. *Gecko will be pleased, Carson will be spared and my job will be safe. I'll ask Gecko to turn over the incriminating photos of Carson and me.* He smiled to himself and said out loud, "I've earned it."

* * * * *

Thorn decided to contact Sophie. *"Sophie?"* he thought.

After a few minutes, he sensed her presence.

"Yes. I'm here. Is everything all right?"

"I'm not sure. Hunter won't let me make a phone call until we get to Russia, so I don't know what's happening back at the office. I can sense Carol is angry, but I haven't been able to talk to her."

Thorn sensed Sophie smile. *"Send her love. She'll be okay."*

Thorn changed the subject. *"Did you know that Chapman tried to buy my cooperation by offering me his daughter?"*

"Yes."

"I don't trust him. He goes out of his way to offer to help me, leads me on with this 'keep the faith' talk and then reneges on every

deal he offers. He's a walking hypocrite. He says he wants stability and when it happens, he changes his mind."

Thorn could sense Sophie wanted to share something with him, but was reluctant.

He thought, *"He has all the money anyone could want at his beck and call. Why would someone with everything going for him single me out for abuse?"*

"Money's not everything."

"But he also has power and influence. I helped do all the things he claimed he wanted done. Instead of following through on what he promised, he stabs me in the back."

Thorn interpreted Sophie's silence as a hint that he should give this more thought.

As he reflected, a thought popped into his head. *"No! Don't tell me that he never really wanted peace and stability, in the first place!"* He paused, his anger growing. *"He was lying to me from the beginning, wasn't he? Pretending to want stability, but secretly wanting chaos!"*

"Not exactly," she thought.

"What do you mean?" he asked, still fuming at his being duped by Chapman. He could sense there was something more she was withholding, something else she wanted him to figure out. It had to do with Erica. *"What does he have to do with Erica?"*

"Erica is his daughter," thought Sophie.

"What? Hunter told me she was the daughter of an Argentine general. Chapman lives in New York."

"That's true. But Chapman is her real father."

Thorn paused to consider the implications. *"That's the daughter he wanted me to marry? Is this some sick joke?"*

Sophie kept silent to give Thorn a chance to calm down.

"If Hunter didn't know this, then no one knows."

"True. Chapman only told her recently."

Thorn paused again. *"Is that why he turned against me? Because I stopped his daughter?"*

"No. You did everything perfectly. No one got hurt, not even his daughter. And even he recognized that she had to be stopped."

"Then why didn't he stop her before she went so far? He must have been monitoring her."

"He wanted to manipulate the situation for as long as he could, before stopping her. Some of what she was doing was useful to him."

"How is extorting money from NATO useful?"

"He only wanted them to agree to the deal so he could use it against the principals later. He didn't want her to actually get the money."

"It sounds like a dangerous game to be playing."

"Eventually, he tried to stop her, but he discovered that he wasn't as powerful as he thought. When he discovered he couldn't put out the fire, but that you could, he was relieved. You saved him from a much greater problem than you could have ever imagined."

"That's why he offered his daughter to me? So he could saddle me with a maniac that he couldn't control himself?" Thorn paused. "Every time I try to put my experiences with Chapman behind me, he does something to open the wound," he thought. "You tell me that my assistance to him was even greater than I knew. Then why does he persecute me?"

"You said it yourself. You **did** everything he was **trying** to do," Sophie thought.

"You're saying he's envious of me?" he asked, not quite convinced.

"Yes. And though he does not know it, he is here to teach you a lesson."

Thorn considered her thoughts and remembered the approval he received for not resorting to violence against his tormentor. "What lesson?"

"It is the most difficult lesson for anyone to master."

Thorn thought for a moment, but didn't acknowledge he understood what she was talking about. He imagined it would be possible to forgive Erica's attacks against him because she didn't know any better. *But would it be possible to forgive someone who pretended to be a man of God? Someone who consciously and knowingly lied for selfish reasons? Was it possible to forgive an arrogant hypocrite who judged others and punished them for refusing to bow down to him?* Thorn felt his stomach turn as he pictured Chapman. *Indeed,* he realized, *forgiveness has to be the most difficult lesson to learn.*

68

△△△

BACK AT THE RUSSIAN military base at Novaya Zemlya, Thorn stood in the doorway of the makeshift laboratory that housed the mockup of the suitcase nuclear device. The stark white walls high-lighted the fact that this was not a place to relax, but rather a solemn place where serious topics were discussed. He watched as Hunter handed the lead box containing the plutonium core to Yuri, the nuclear scientist who had instructed him on how to dis-arm it. Standing next to the scientist was his large Russian friend, the military commander who'd arranged for Yuri's briefing two days earlier. "Thanks for your help. I hope you didn't need the rest of it," Hunter said with a slight, wry smile. "We were in a hurry."

The scientist laughed. "No. Without fissile material, you can't make a bomb. No matter *how* many nuclear experts you put in a room."

"What happened to the truck convoy?" Hunter asked the military commander.

"We tracked them all the way to Karachi. An informant with Pakistan Inter-Services Intelligence indicated the device was headed to Boston. Your government was notified."

"It can't do any damage anyway," Hunter replied. "By the way, I need to use a secure phone. Can you help me out with that?"

Thorn watched as Hunter's Russian friend directed him to an office outside the laboratory and pointed to a phone. After punch-ing in a series of numbers, he spoke loudly into the phone, "Vega, this is Hunter."

"Do you know what time it is?" a gruff voice with a slight His-panic accent boomed back at him.

"I don't care," chided Hunter. "Did you get the video?"

"Is this line secure?" the voice questioned.

"Yes it's secure and no, you won't be able to trace the call," Hunter responded. "Quit stalling. Did you get the video?"

"Yes."

"Good. Then you understand what happened?" Hunter asked.

"Apparently."

"Okay, put me through to Miller."

After a brief pause, Hunter was connected with the Director of Central Intelligence. As soon as Miller's voice came on the line, Hunter growled, "Call off your *damn* agents! You heard it from Vega. Hawke framed me. It's all on the goddamn videotaped confession."

"Did you torture him?"

"No . . . well, maybe a little. But he deserved it," said Hunter. "Are you going to try to justify having your agents follow me or are you going to shut up so I can tell you where Hawke and Buenavista are?"

"Go ahead," Miller said, keen on locating the duo.

Thorn smiled as Hunter continued with his conversation. He glanced at the Russian who was grinning ear-to-ear. After Hunter gave Miller the terrorists' current whereabouts, he hung up and turned to Thorn. "Okay, your turn."

"Thanks." He took the phone from Hunter and dialed Carol's cell phone number.

"Hello?" he heard her say, a slight crackle in the line.

"Hi, Carol. It's Alec."

Thorn held the receiver away from his ear. He could still hear her yelling at him. "Where are you? Why didn't you call? What's wrong with you?"

Hunter smiled and whispered loudly, "You really have a way with women, Thorn."

Ignoring the jab, Thorn tried calming her down by speaking softly, "Please, Carol, I apologize. I'll explain everything when I see you." Quickly changing the subject, he asked, "What happened with Tachyon?"

"You've got a meeting with the President at 9 AM tomorrow."

"Where?" he asked.

"The Holiday Inn in Highland Beach."

"The Holiday Inn?" Thorn asked. "I'm not in the area." He looked at Hunter and covered the mouthpiece. "What's the chance we get back to Florida tomorrow by 9 AM?"

"What's so important?"

"My company. You know, the one whose future I threw away when I went with you to Pakistan."

"Well, if you put it that way," Hunter said. He checked his watch. "We can make it if we leave now."

Thorn returned to Carol. "I'll meet you at the Holiday Inn in Highland Beach at 9 AM."

"You'll have to go by yourself. I'm already in New York with Steve and Hans. We're scheduled to meet at Tachyon's headquarters to make sure the systems can be integrated."

"Okay, fine," he said. "I'll take care of my end and you coordinate the technical issues up in New York."

"You'll be there?" she asked apprehensively.

"Yes," Thorn replied, "I'll be there. Don't worry."

* * * * *

Erica sat up on her cot when she heard the slide of the deadbolt and saw the door swing open. A slightly built man with steel-rimmed glasses entered, looking more like an accountant than a jailer. She could make out the slight bulge under his jacket that indicated a concealed weapon.

"Miss Buenavista, I'm Mr. House," he said, offering his hand in greeting. "Mr. Chapman sent me to obtain your release."

Erica shook his hand. "Where are we?" she asked.

"Reston, Virginia," he replied. "I've been asked to accompany you on the first flight from Dulles up to New York. Mr. Chapman said you'd understand."

She nodded, impressed with Chapman's influence. She had agreed to contact him after she was freed. He had arranged to act as a sort of parole officer for her. No charges would be filed, if she complied with the conditions he'd established in his negotiations with the government. She doubted it was legal, but it didn't matter. She had no intention of following any orders that she herself didn't originate.

"Follow me," said Mr. House as he began leading her down a long, narrow, concrete hallway. "I'm parked right outside the front gate."

Exiting the prison with this thin, unassuming man at her side, she stood for a moment outside the main gate, drew in a deep breath, let it out slowly, and blinked in the bright sunlight.

* * * * *

Thorn was sleeping on the plane when he sensed that someone needed his help. He was conscious that it was Sophie, while he continued to dream.

In his dream, he recognized the Cleric's stepson was chasing Sophie. Thorn positioned his astral body between the young man and Sophie. He quickly maneuvered himself so that Sophie was behind him, keeping her out of striking distance.

"You are the one responsible for shutting off our funding!" yelled the young man. *"You don't care at all about my people!"*

"You're wrong!" Thorn barked back at him. The hatred in the man's eyes told Thorn that rational argument was not about to work against his impassioned tirade.

Without warning, Thorn lunged forward and grabbed the young man, who resisted like a cat not wanting to take a bath. Thorn momentarily lost his grip before he has able to pin the man's arms in a half nelson. He then waited until the young man stopped his contortions. Drawing raw spiritual energy through his crown chakra, Thorn quickly bathed himself and the Cleric's son in its tranquilizing force.

As soon as Thorn loosened his grip, the young man broke away and turned to face him. Thorn looked directly into his eyes and could see some of the hatred he'd felt earlier had dissipated. The young man's look was one of questioning, more than distrust. After briefly gazing at Thorn's compassionate face, the man literally disappeared from the scene. Thorn turned back to Sophie to see if she was all right.

"Yes, I'm fine," she thought.

"Why was he chasing you?"

"He wanted you, but couldn't find you. So he used me to get your attention."

"I get the feeling that this encounter and the one in the mansion were both a lot more important than I originally estimated." He paused, confused by the feelings that came over him.

"It may take him a while to understand what you did, but some day he'll realize that you helped him," Sophie thought.

Thorn swallowed hard as he recognized what he had accomplished. *"I tried to do what God would have wanted me to do."*

Sophie thought, *"To place your will completely in line with that of God is the example that Jesus set for others to follow. It is also what the word Islam means: 'surrender to the will of God.'"*

Thorn remained silent, thankful to God that he had been successful in overpowering the emotional firebrand until he calmed down. He prayed that he would be worthy of the power he had been given.

* * * * *

As they drove through Reston on their way to Dulles Airport, House answered Erica's question the same way he answered each of her previous questions, "Mr. Chapman will explain."

She pointed to a Walgreens Drug store and said, "I've got a headache. Do you mind if we stop for some aspirin?"

House pulled over. "We need to hurry or we'll miss our flight."

Erica entered with House trailing. Careful to use her body as a shield, she grabbed a roll of duct tape as she walked down the office supplies aisle. She stuck it under her shirt, tucking it into the top of her pants and continued to the back of the store. After picking up a bottle of Tylenol and a bottle of Diet Coke, she returned to the front counter. House paid for the items.

"Okay?" he asked, watching her wash down two capsules with the soda outside the store.

"I just need a restroom and I'll be set," she said. "I saw one around back." She turned the corner and walked away.

House followed her. "There's no restroom back there."

"Right here," she said, as she walked past the dumpster.

"Where are you going?" he asked coming around.

She spun around and met him with a knee. She took his gun from the holster under his jacket while he was doubled over. "Do what I say and you won't be hurt any worse."

She helped him limp to the car and said, "Get in and drive. We're going to Florida."

69

△△△

There are no mistakes, no coincidences. All events are blessings given to us to learn from.
—Elizabeth Kubler-Ross

ERICA ROSE FROM her bed and entered the shower. She smiled at what she'd accomplished in such a short time. It hadn't been much of an effort to steal House's gun, money and car. He even wore the kind of Ray Ban sunglasses she liked. She'd left him in the woods off a rural highway in Georgia, tied up with duct tape. *No need to kill him,* she thought to herself—*after all, he did work for my father.* She knew he'd be found in a couple of hours. After dropping him off, she'd driven to another safe house in Boynton Beach, six miles north of Boca Raton.

Exiting the shower, Erica checked herself in the mirror. Except for the rings under her eyes, she noted that she didn't look too bad, considering that she'd only had three hours of sleep. Makeup would hide the rings. She wanted to look her best when she killed Thorn.

* * * * *

Thorn checked his watch—8 AM. He knew they were close to landing, this time near Lake Okeechobee in Palm Beach County. Hunter broke the silence. "Your Mazda rental car will be waiting for you at the landing strip. Also, a change of clothes."

"*My* rental car?"

"Yeah. I had one of my men move it."

"Without my keys?" asked Thorn playfully.

"My men don't need keys."

Hunter landed the plane on the short runway used by the owner of the sugar plantation. As soon as they'd taxied over to the corrugated metal, makeshift hangar, Thorn climbed out the cockpit and stood on the wing. He turned to Hunter, "Thanks for driving. Remind me never to do anything this stupid in the future."

Hunter smiled. "You're welcome. I'm sorry I can't come with you, but I need to stash this baby," he said, patting the stealth fighter. "I want to hear how you're going to explain where you've been."

Thorn smiled. "Good question." He hung off the wing and dropped to the ground.

Hunter called to him. "Here. Take this," throwing down a black, plastic handgun.

"What's this?"

"It's the Glock from the black ops guy."

"That's just what I need—a stolen gun."

"That gun doesn't exist, so it can't be stolen," said Hunter. "Just keep it with you. It might come in handy."

Thorn picked it up to humor Hunter. "All right."

Thorn saw the Mazda amongst the sugar cane and said, "I've gotta' go. Thanks."

He stuck the Glock under the spare shirt Hunter's man had left on the passenger seat. He'd change later. With an hour to get to the meeting, Thorn turned onto Route 27 and headed south. The narrow two-lane road was, thankfully, free of traffic. Taking a deep breath, he leaned back comfortably into the driver's seat, gazing quietly through the windshield. Suddenly, a bad feeling overcame him.

Thorn tried to identify the source, but could only sense that someone was angry with him. He focused on Carol and immediately discounted her as being the one. She was anxious, he recognized, but not angry.

He cycled through a list of people who might be responsible and stopped when he came to Erica. He sensed she was enraged and planning to make him pay for it. Thorn shook his head, wondering why she always got so worked up over him.

He dismissed her from his mind, knowing she was in government custody. *They are not about to let a terrorist loose.* He focused on her intentions. *She wants revenge.* He sighed and tried to put it out of his mind. He had a business to run.

* * * * *

Erica Buenavista left the safe house and drove south on A1A alongside the ocean. She ignored the palm trees, the well-manicured golf course and the ocean views, as she sped along in Mr. House's black Lincoln Town Car. She was busy rehearsing in her mind how she would deal with Thorn. *Shooting him would not be enough,* she mused. *He must suffer. Know what it is to fear. Feel what it's like to be humiliated. When he's resigned to die, I'll give him a glimmer of hope. Just enough so that he'll thank me for sparing his life and praise my greatness. Then, I'll kill him*

* * * * *

Traffic was light as Thorn drove east on Atlantic Avenue in Delray Beach. Thorn's ominous feelings persisted. When his cell phone rang, he saw Carol's number and answered it, hoping she would take his mind off Erica. "Yes, Carol."

"Where are you?" she asked.

"Delray," he said, laughing. "Did you think I wouldn't get back in time?"

"You haven't been that punctual, lately," she said. Thorn could hear her sigh with relief.

"What about you? When's your meeting?" he asked.

"Not until 10 AM. We're having breakfast at Windows on the World . . . and yes, I *am* enjoying the view."

He tried to smile, but his sense of approaching doom wouldn't leave.

She said, "I just wanted to make sure you got there. Are you all right?" She paused, then somewhat more softly added, "I have to admit, Alec, I've been *worried* about you."

Her tone of voice, certainly more heartfelt than normal, caught him off guard. "Well, yeah, I'm here," he said.

She remained silent, hoping he would continue.

"Carol, I . . ."

"Yes . . .?" she asked trying to get him to open up.

"I . . . we—well, . . . we can talk about it, when you get back to Florida," he managed to say. "Good luck with your meeting. Call me later, okay?" He hung up before she could respond.

"Shit!" he said aloud, disappointed that he blew his opportunity to talk to her in a social context. *I just helped disarm a nuclear device and I'm too scared to ask an awesome woman to dinner. What's wrong with this picture?* Alec took a deep breath and exhaled his frustration, as he returned his attention to the task at hand.

He continued driving past the restaurants and small shops on Atlantic Avenue, places he'd enjoyed stopping into for years. Checking his watch again, he noted that he had half an hour to spare. *Plenty of time to freshen up and change,* he happily thought to himself. *I'll reassure Tachyon's president to do the deal and the company will be saved.*

Thorn drew in a slow, deep breath and forced himself to focus on his meeting. *The meeting will go well,* he confidently thought. *An alliance with Tachyon makes good business sense.* In the back of his mind, though, a dark feeling kept nagging away at him. *Hate and revenge,* he sensed. It was now thoroughly distracting him. He stopped at the light at A1A and closed his eyes. He couldn't get rid of it.

Thorn watched as the light turned green and then waited as the last car zipped through to beat the light. He blinked his eyes in disbelief—it was Erica!

He dismissed his thought, knowing for certain that she was locked up. He turned south and continued on down the narrow two-lane road. Traffic began to back up just as he crossed over into Highland Beach, as a vehicle ahead waited to make a left turn. Slowly, Thorn closed in on the same car that beat the light.

He tried to calm his mind, as a thousand thoughts ran through it. *Was it really Erica?* His mind said "no," but his intuition told him it was. *Does she know I'm following her? Unlikely,* he thought. *She wouldn't expect me to be traveling south. She's too preoccupied to notice, anyway.*

He locked onto her mind and could sense her anxiety. *What could it be that has her on edge? Can't tell.* He took a deep breath. *Is she going to the Holiday Inn? Does she know about my meeting? Unlikely. It's just a coincidence. But . . . there are no coincidences.*

Time slowed down as his mind raced. The Holiday Inn was now only a minute away. *Should I slow down and let her drive away? Should I turn off before she sees me? What about my meeting? It could decide the future of my company. What should I do?*

He kept driving. After a few more blocks, Thorn watched her twist the rearview mirror down to check her appearance. Satisfied, she readjusted her mirror. He watched as she paused ever so slightly. *She knows I'm behind her.* But Thorn could tell that she was not expecting him, even through her dark sunglasses.

Slowing down, she turned right into the rest area on the Intracoastal Waterway across from the Holiday Inn and eased the Lincoln into an angled parking space facing the water. Time seemed to expand as Thorn slowed his car; each tire revolution seemed to take forever, giving him ample time to think: *The investors are waiting for me inside the Holiday Inn. Will she follow me if I go in? Is this a set-up? Does she want to kill me? Will she shoot me in the lobby? If I continue straight, she'll follow and I'll lose the deal with Tachyon.* Thorn continued to drive as he gazed over at Erica with the entire world acting in slow motion.

Underneath the spare shirt on the passenger seat was the Glock that Hunter had given him. *Should I take it?* He reached for it and stopped. He could hear Sophie's voice. *"You don't need a gun."*

Instinctively, Thorn knew to take the offensive, turning right into the rest area and parking next to Erica. He observed her through his open passenger window, sensing her confusion. Having made his decision, time seemed to return to normal.

She quickly scanned the area, and, spotting no one, exited her car. Smiling with well-practiced social grace, she greeted Alec. "Hello, Thorn. What a coincidence running into you here. How are you?"

"Great," he said, continuing to hold her gaze.

"I was just driving down the street, trying to get some fresh air. What brings you out?" she asked.

"I was looking for you," he replied, the words coming out without pause. Thorn could sense her confusion, but she did not betray herself with any physical actions. She was sizing up the situation.

"Would you like to go for coffee? There's a hotel across the street," she said, suspicious that this might be a setup.

"Sure."

"Let me get my purse," she said, leaning into her car with her back to Thorn.

Thorn put his hand around the Glock underneath the shirt. He could hear Sophie's voice again, this time more immediate, *"You don't need a gun."*

He got out of the car, leaving the gun on the front seat. He walked with her across the street into the lobby of the Holiday Inn, which was empty, except for the incessant blather of a wall-mounted TV. He turned it off before they sat down, facing each other.

"Why were you looking for me?" she asked.

"I wanted to ask you, 'Why?'"

"Why what?"

Thorn kept quiet a moment, letting his silence convey that he was not interested in another big lie. "Why you did the things you did over the past several months?"

Thorn watched as she scanned him. She said, "I don't know what you mean."

Thorn sighed, recognizing that she intended to stick with the big lie strategy. "I was hoping you might acknowledge your errors and start making amends."

"I don't know what you're talking about."

Thorn stared at her and, without opening his mouth, conveyed his belief that she was lying and that if she weren't wearing any dark glasses, her eyes would betray her. She took off her Ray Bans. "See. Look at my eyes," she said.

Thorn looked and grew sad. Her blue-gray eyes could not hide her lies. Rather than the clear eyes of a healthy person, her eyes revealed the torture of her campaigns to control him and the world. Cracks ran from her pupils to the sides of each eye. He was not relying on his inner vision to view the pain. It was physically evident.

Uncomfortable with Thorn's stare, she stood up to leave. He could sense her thoughts. *Something is wrong,* she thought. *Better to kill him later.* She began to walk away.

Thorn stood up and called after her, "Didn't anyone ever tell you never send a raven to trim the wings of an eagle?"

She turned towards him, her face filled with rage. "I had forgotten why I had to kill you. I'm glad you reminded me." She reached into her purse and took out House's gun, aiming it at Thorn.

Thorn sat down. He knew his comment would incite her. "Now we're getting somewhere," he said in a matter-of-fact tone.

Thorn watched as Erica scrutinized him. He could sense her confusion. *I'm the one with the gun,* she thought. *I'm the one in control, but . . . he's not showing any fear.* She gritted her teeth together, before she decided, *He must learn fear.* "Any last thoughts before you die?" she asked.

Thorn kept silent.

She cocked the gun and in a taunting voice, asked. "Would you like to beg for mercy?"

Thorn remained silent. He peered deeply into her eyes. In front of him, he saw a little girl standing alone who wanted to be somebody important. He could feel the pain that she had brought upon herself, as well as that of her previous victims. He closed his eyes. Slowly, waves of anguish flowed through his body. Feelings of isolation, fear, hatred and hopelessness filled him. Thorn breathed deeply to take in spiritual energy, to flush these poisons from his being.

Thorn lost track of time as he focused on the toxins. The more he tried to flush them from his system, the more they seemed to multiply and grow in intensity. The spiritual energy, which normally would flow freely through his body, seemed to flow slowly, as if it were passing through thick sludge. He willed the cleansing energy through his body, visualizing a high-pressure hose unrelentingly washing it away. Initially, it started as a tight narrow band, but slowly, he expanded the hose's diameter, while maintaining its intensity.

Gradually, the spiritual energy began flowing faster and faster, until, at last, he sensed he was clear of her negative energy.

Slowly, he opened his eyes and a single tear ran down his face. Erica was no longer pointing the gun at him. He recognized that she was aware of what he saw. A huge burden had been lifted from her being. She fought to maintain her stoic demeanor, which kept her from crying, but the hard crust protecting her from feeling emotion had been removed.

"I wanted to tell you that I forgive you," he said.

Thorn watched her mouth open and close without speaking. He could sense the hatred had drained out of her and could see in her face, unmistakably, that she recognized the gift he had given her—a gift much more valuable than revenge or his life.

Thorn inquired of her, "Is there anything you'd like to ask me?"

Still shaken by the experience, she shook her head "no."

"Good luck," he said, getting up.

"Stop," she demanded, regaining her composure. "I'm not done with you, yet."

Thorn sat down again. She sat across from him.

"Where's my bomb?"

"The last I heard, it was on its way to Boston, minus the plutonium. That's back in Russia."

She kept her breathing even, but Thorn could feel the rage building in her once again. He locked into her, as before, but could sense that she was losing control. He closed his eyes and flushed his and her body with more highly focused, intense spiritual energy. Thorn realized, though, that he couldn't break her out of her cycle of rage. The sound of a hotel guest snapped him into full wakefulness.

"Oh my God!" cried the middle-aged woman. She was carrying a cell phone and rushed towards the TV to turn it on. In full color, was the replay of a large airplane crashing into the South Tower of the World Trade Center. The North Tower was already aflame.

The announcer's voice said, "United Airlines Flight 175, on route from Boston to Los Angeles . . ."

Thorn's mind went blank. All he could focus on was the word "Boston." A sense of knowing came over him, as he locked eyes with Erica. Without having to say a word, he saw that she also understood.

He closed his eyes and the visions came—the alternate future. The one in which Erica's nuclear device did not get disarmed. The one where it was transported to Boston and loaded on Flight 175. The one where it exploded upon contact with the South Tower. He looked at the TV, but the images he saw were in his mind. A giant mushroom cloud, followed by fireballs that incinerated all of lower Manhattan. Hundreds of thousands dead instantly. Millions more expected to die slowly of radiation sickness.

Numbed by his revelation, Thorn turned to Erica. Their eyes locked and he could see that she understood also. Now able to feel emotion, she was identifying with the pain of everyone who died, as well as the millions who died in the alternate future. And she understood that without Thorn and Hunter's intervention, she would have been partly responsible. She turned away from Thorn, shamed and unable to meet his gaze. Within just a few moments, Erica got up and left.

He returned his focus to the physical world. And then he remembered Carol. Frantically, he took out his cell phone and dialed her number. *Voice Mail! No*, he thought, *her phone is turned off! Windows on the World—which tower was it in?* He paused briefly and remembered—*the North Tower! The one already on fire.*

Quickly, Thorn clicked the keys on his cell phone to find his head developer's number. He pressed the talk key and held his breath while it rang.

"Hello, Alec," came the weak reply from Hans. "Carol told us to meet her in the lobby. She was going to surprise her brother who works for some insurance company on the 83rd floor." His voice began to crack. "We don't know where she is. It's a madhouse."

"Okay," Thorn said. "Let me go." He hung up.

With the TV showing replay after replay of the two crashes and amid the shocked hotel guests, Thorn sat back in the lobby chair, closed his eyes again and tuned out the distractions. He pictured Carol in his mind. She was lying alone, motionless on the floor. *Is she dead?* he wondered. Without thinking he was floating above her. The pitch-black hallway was filled with smoke. With his inner senses, he could smell burning jet fuel and various chemicals. He floated down from the ceiling and tried to rouse her, but his hands passed right through her. He yelled, *"Wake up,"* but she didn't respond. He pleaded with her, *"Please, get up. You have to get out."* Still no response.

"You have to wake up. How else can I tell you that 'I love you'?" His words surprised even him, but he had no time to think. *"Yes, I love you. Now, I realize it. Please, wake up so I can tell you in person."* He opened his heart and projected love and energy into her body. *"Please, please, pleeeeease . . ."*

"Alec?" she asked.

The sound of her voice jolted him back into his body in the hotel lobby. Quickly he focused on her and returned to the hallway. *"Yes. I'm here."*

"I can't see you," she said, as she began choking on the fumes.

"Don't worry, I'm with you." He floated down the hallway until he sensed a stairwell just around the corner. He returned to her side. *"Stay low, Carol. Crawl."* He projected an image of her crawling into her head. Within seconds, she began to crawl forward. *"Keep going,"* he encouraged her. *"Just a little farther."*

"Stay with me," she said.

"Yes, I'm with you. I won't leave you. I promise." He paused and allowed himself, for a moment, to really experience what he felt for her, how much he'd grown to appreciate her, to love her. A moment later, he told her, *"Keep moving."* Slowly she made it down the hall and around the corner. A rolled up newspaper propped the stairwell door partially open. *"Put your hand on the wall. Feel for the door."* Her hands swept along the wall feeling for the door. When she grasped it, he ordered, *"That's it. Pull it open."*

He could tell she was pulling, but was unable to open the door. *"It's too heavy."*

"You can do it. Put your legs against the wall and pull the door open."

He watched as she repositioned herself, lying on the floor, her black pumps against the door jam. With her two hands, she slowly opened the door.

"Now, slide through the door before it springs shut again." She kicked her way through as her shoe came off and tumbled down the stairwell.

"Hello?" boomed a deep voice from below. "Is anybody up there?"

"Yes," yelled Carol, before another coughing spasm silenced her.

A firefighter slowly ascended the stairs, which were dimly lit by the emergency lights. "Come with me!" he hollered. Recognizing she was unable to walk, he picked her up and hoisted her on his shoulder.

"Wait," she ordered. "Alec is here with me."

The fireman looked around the empty stairwell and pushed open the fire door. "Hello," he yelled into the hallway. "Alec? Anybody?" He waited a few seconds for a response. "There's no one here," said the firefighter. "We need to go. Now!"

"But—"

"Go!" yelled Alec silently to Carol. *"Don't worry about me."*

"Alec?" she thought puzzled.

"It's okay. I'm safe," he thought. *"And yes, I do love you."*

She smiled before losing consciousness. The fireman raced down the stairs. Alec returned to his body.

70

△ △ △

And when you pray, do not be like the hypocrites, for they love to pray standing in the synagogues and on the street corners to be seen by men. I tell you the truth, they have received their reward in full.

—Matthew 6:5

TACHYON'S PRESIDENT, Brent Hall, waited for Thorn to carefully read over the term sheet his lawyer had prepared. As soon as Thorn looked up, Hall asked, "Are there any provisions you'd like me to explain?"

"No, it's pretty straightforward," replied Thorn, placing the term sheet on the table. "Basically, you want to buy the whole company and keep me on to run things. The actual price you pay would depend on us attaining certain goals."

"That's right. For accounting reasons, it's best we acquire 100% of the stock."

"Can we set things up so that my employees would get to share in the future profits of the company?"

"Certainly," answered Hall. "We like the idea of compensation tied to performance—including yours."

"I appreciate that. But what if I was to leave? Could I ensure my employees would still be retained and that they'd be able to share in the future profits of the division?"

Hall stared at Thorn with his mouth agape, before he managed to say, "I don't understand. I thought overseeing this company's growth was what you wanted to do."

"It was," Thorn replied. "But things have changed." He hesitated. "It's a big world out there. I need to see it."

Hall continued to stare at Thorn.

"Don't worry," Thorn said. "I can set things up to make sure every goal is attained—the value of my stock depends on it. But after that, I'd like to move on."

Hall nodded his agreement, still slightly dumbfounded at Thorn's changed attitude.

"One last point," Thorn said. "I'd like to give Carol a month off with full pay, to allow her to recover from her ordeal."

"That's perfectly understandable."

"Then we have a deal," Thorn said, as he stood up to shake hands with Hall. "Have your attorney draft the documents. Any questions, you can reach me on my cell."

Thorn walked out the door and climbed into his red Mazda Protégé rental car. Starting up the engine, he put it in gear and headed to New York to visit Carol.

* * * * *

Thorn was waiting at Carol's bedside when she awoke. She smiled at him when her eyes regained their focus. "You didn't have to drive all the way here to New York. That wasn't necessary."

"It was *very* necessary," he responded. "How're you feeling?"

"Fine," she answered. "I banged my head when I tripped in the dark, but it's just a bump."

Thorn nodded, remembering how she seemed unconscious when he viewed her while out of his body. "How's your brother?"

"Thank God, he was out of town that day," she replied.

"Do you feel like talking about it, or is it too early?"

"I've already discussed it with the doctors. They want to be sure I'm not still in shock, but I feel okay."

"Maybe they're right," Thorn offered, though skeptical of their diagnosis.

"An odd thing happened during my experience." She scanned his eyes wondering if she should go on. "The doctors explained that it was caused by a lack of oxygen to my brain—hypoxia. Basically, I was hallucinating."

"Really?" he asked. "Tell me what happened," he said, holding back a smile. He looked at her with eyes that signaled he would understand.

"It's a little embarrassing, but I guess I can tell you."

Thorn waited for her to continue.

"I felt like you were with me in the hallway up on the 83rd floor." She looked carefully at him to gauge his reaction. "I know it sounds weird, but you were encouraging me to keep moving and get out. I could hear you clearly. You even told me how to open the stairwell door."

Thorn smiled. "Was that before or after I said 'I love you'?"

Her eyes locked on his, but this time she wasn't afraid. "You *were* there," she gasped.

"Yes," he nodded. "And when I said I wouldn't leave you, I wasn't kidding. I'm not—that is, if it's okay with you."

Thorn watched her eyes begin to moisten. She motioned for him to come closer and embraced him when he leaned over her. "Yes, it's okay with me," she cooed. "I love you, too."

He kissed her tenderly, before he straightened up again. "It's best you don't tell the doctors about this. They won't discharge you if you're still 'hallucinating.'"

She laughed, then became serious. "But how is it possible?"

"There's a lot to tell you, but we have plenty of time. We're not expected back at the office for a month. A little R&R is what Dr. Alec Thorn prescribes."

"The doctors that sign the forms said I could leave tomorrow."

"I guess I can wait," he joked, knowing he was right where he wanted to be.

* * * * *

Thorn checked into the Sheraton on 47th Street in Manhattan to spend the night. Relieved that Carol was okay, another question troubled him. *"Why did all those people have to die?"* He didn't want someone on TV to tell him. He didn't care about their opinions. He wanted the truth.

Lying down on his king-sized bed, he took several deep breaths, simultaneously flushing his body with spiritual energy. He could feel prickly sensations on the crown of his head, as he sought the highest wisdom available to him—the link to his oversoul.

Now relaxed, he visualized the burning towers. Feelings of sadness welled up in him that were so intense he grimaced. He pinpointed the source of these feelings—they came from the survivors, and the friends, coworkers and loved ones of the people who died. They too wanted to understand, "Why?"

The agony filling his emotional body prevented him from contacting the ones who passed on. Knowing he had to dispel the negativity, he embraced the pain and sadness, fully experienced it, before he released it through his crown chakra, asking God to take it away. Unburdened of his pain, he now had a clear, direct connection to his oversoul.

In his mind's eye, he could now see many of the people who had perished in the disaster and was surprised to be filled with intense feelings of love—not fear. Some of the people who died wanted to communicate their feelings. Thorn heard them clearly:

They did it out of love—not fear. They chose to die. They are in a better place. They want everyone on earth to know this. There are many levels to this drama. At the physical level, it was allowed to happen. To start a war. To manipulate people's emotions. To keep humanity in bondage. Have compassion, but do not retaliate. It was necessary. Do not seek revenge. Do not be afraid. If humanity can overcome this, it will advance far in its development.

Thorn opened his eyes and wrote down these thoughts before he forgot them. He saw the pattern. Erica and Chapman had sought to control and manipulate him. Their motivations were selfish. And yet, they had forced him to develop new spiritual muscles. He could do things he would never have dreamed possible just a few months earlier. The terrorist act was intended to do the same. The ones responsible had selfish motives, but the end result would advance humanity.

The future is not set in stone, he reflected. *A nuclear holocaust has been prevented and so can other horrible events. To change the future, people must decide what type of future they want. Either they choose to remain passive victims and allow others to tell them what to think and feel, or they choose to express their God-given gifts in harmony with others. When enough choose the latter, the fear and hate mongers will be swept aside and the world will evolve.*

Every individual must choose; every one could become a mystic warrior.

He felt a large weight lift from his being and the lingering feelings of sadness dissolve. He felt bad for all the people who lost loved ones. But now, at least, it made sense. They *did* die for a reason. And they were at peace.

* * * * *

Feeling better after his healing meditation, Thorn sat relaxing in the hotel room's recliner. This time, he focused on the positive events of the past few weeks. Without realizing it, he projected his thoughts, *"How ironic. On the one hand . . . is a bounty hunter, who risks his life and disobeys his government to disarm a nuclear bomb. On the other hand . . . is a self-proclaimed 'man of God,' who deceives and destroys anyone who disagrees with him."*

Thorn sensed that he was not alone in his thoughts. In his mind's eye, he saw the smiling face of Jesus.

"Are you wondering which one is the Good Samaritan?" Jesus asked.

Smiling, Thorn replied, *"In one of my exchanges with Chapman, I used a quote that—"*

"About the speck in your eye?"

"I guess it's not necessary for me to finish my thoughts."

"Did you think that hypocrites only existed 2000 years ago? Did you think it was my intention that the lessons I taught should be locked in a book and never used?"

Thorn smiled again.

"Besides," Jesus thought, *"where do you think you got the idea to use that quote?"*

"I'm not religious," Thorn thought. *"I don't even go to church."*

"When you pray, do not be like the hypocrites who love to pray standing in the house of God to be seen by men. Pray when you are alone. Your Father will know what you need before you even ask."

"In my meditations, I sense that there are many more beings that I can now contact. How will I know the good from the bad?"

"You will know them by their fruit," Jesus thought and then silently faded from Thorn's mind.

* * * * *

It was well after midnight. Unable to sleep, Thorn chose to meditate. He cleared his mind and took several deep breaths, while he cleansed his spiritual bodies. He needed to talk to God.

"Thank you God for granting me these blessings. I'm grateful that you gave me the strength and the power to save Carol and to overcome those who sought to destroy me. And to help prevent an even worse disaster from occurring."

Feeling satisfied with his expression of gratitude, he pondered how he should phrase the next part of his prayer. *"God, I also want to forgive Erica and Chapman for what they did to me. I hope they will use their abilities to help others, instead of seeking power solely for their own purposes."*

As Thorn lay in bed, he gradually became aware of energy flowing through the top of his head. The feeling expanded and soon, the entire crown of his head, as well as his forehead, felt as if a fire hose was hooked up to it.

Pictures formed in his mind's eye: clouds rolled in toward him at high-speed, like a movie, only 10 times faster. Darkness descended and lightning struck all around. In the blackened sky, a bald eagle flew swiftly through a thundercloud swollen with rain. Emerging from the massive rainstorm, the eagle soared across the sky and swooped down to perch on a huge live oak. From behind the dark bank of clouds, streaming rays of sunlight began pouring down, as the eagle spread its wings wide. Abruptly, the pictures stopped.

Thorn sat quietly for a long while, reflecting upon the vision he'd just witnessed. Unable to fathom all its significance, he projected himself through his third eye and the top of his head, where the images had seemed to originate.

"God? Are you there? Please explain what you mean by what you showed me."

Thorn waited, hoping for a response. Soon, he felt the same sensation as before; his entire crown and forehead were engulfed in a stream of energy. In addition, he felt his heart beating slowly, rhythmically and with a sense of pure love.

"God, you can hear me?"

In a moment out of time, he suddenly felt the joy of a woman giving birth, understood the wisdom of divine law, experienced the sense of being everywhere and nowhere, and felt the unity of himself with everything. He realized that God was all of these and much more, an essence not to be contemplated, but personally experienced.

Thorn lay back as he felt the connection slowly dissolve. He could feel his body still vibrating with energy and relished the profound joy and humility of this gift.

Sophie's presence came gently to him. He realized that she had been watching. *"You saw what happened?"*

"Yes."

"You can do that?"

"Ever since I was 12."

All his meetings and conversations with her flashed past him in an instant. He understood how she had always been able to provide him such good advice.

"This is the end?" he asked.

"No. The beginning."

* * * * *

Gecko sat on the park bench wondering what had gone wrong. *Only four planes had been hijacked and Europe was unscathed! Worst of all, the nuclear bomb that I had worked so hard to locate for the Cleric did not go off. It was loaded on the plane, yet . . . it was as if some spiritual force had been protecting these mindless sheep.*

Buenavista is to blame. She should have sold the nuclear weapon to the Cleric much earlier. She's weak and unreliable. I will be stronger.

He made himself a commitment to clean up and make due with the damage that was done. *War will be declared and the civil liberties of the sheep will be eliminated. The opportunity to seize overt control would have to wait.*

Gecko looked up and saw White approaching. He rose from the park bench and forced himself to smile, gesturing that they should take a walk. White was smiling.

"Everything is completely erased," he said. "There's no record of anything that happened in Pakistan for the past week."

"You're sure?" asked Gecko.

"Absolutely. I duplicated a loop from another time period and placed it in the archives. No one would suspect a thing."

"Excellent work," said Gecko, as he stopped in the shadows of the cherry trees. Gecko nodded, as a jogger with a baggy sweatshirt approached from behind.

"Did you bring the negatives?" asked White. "That was our agreement."

"Yes, of course," he said, as he watched White's eyes grow bright. Gecko listened to the sound of two bullets muffled by a silencer escape from the jogger's gun. White's bright eyes glassed over and he crumpled to the ground.

Gecko watched the jogger drag White's body into the undergrowth before walking impassively out of the park.

Epilogue

△ △ △

As above, so below.
—Hermes Trimegistus

THORN SAT MEDITATING near the top of Waimoku Falls on East Maui before dawn. Deep in thought, he was oblivious to the sound of the water cascading down Mount Haleakala and to the rich smells of the lush foliage that surrounded him. Blissfully content, he reflected back on the last time he'd sat in this exotic setting.

He smiled serenely, as the memories that he had blocked out for lack of understanding came streaming back. This was where he had first left his body, 25 years earlier. As if on cue, he heard the voice inside his head, *"This is how you travel to distant worlds."*

He was not an eight-year old boy, now. With the wealth of experience and understanding he'd gained, he was no longer limited to space and time—he could travel anywhere.

He focused his attention on the source of the communication. Warm and comfortable. A strong sense of familiarity. He wanted to go there . . . home.

"Do not feel homesick," said the voice. *"I am a part of you. And I am only a thought away."*

The longing vanished and a sense of knowingness returned. Part of him was everywhere and connected to everything. He would never be lonely again.

Slowly, Thorn opened his eyes and returned his focus to the physical world, marveling again at the raw beauty of nature. He watched Carol hiking through the bamboo thicket, slowly moving up the trail to meet him. As he stood up, he thanked God for creating this sacred place and for giving him the opportunity to return.